$\angle\omega$

D1212663

Danger *in* Spades

Elizabeth Penney

Annie's®
AnniesFiction.com

Books in the Antique Shop Mysteries series

Library of Congress-in-Publication Data
Danger in Spades / by Elizabeth Penney
p. cm.
I. Title
                    2017944653

AnniesFiction.com
(800) 282-6643
Antique Shop Mysteries™
Series Creator: Shari Lohner
Series Editor: Elizabeth Morrissey
Cover Illustrator: Bonnie Leick

10 11 12 13 14 | Printed in China | 9 8 7 6 5 4 3

1

$\mathbf{W}$ind howled down the chimney of Sedgwick Manor, making the flames dance in the fireplace. Beyond tall windows framed by velvet curtains, winter trees tossed their branches, trunks bowing before the force of the storm.

Snuggling deeper into the afghan covering her shoulders, Maggie Watson reached out and stroked the tabby cat sprawled on the sofa beside her. "When they coined the phrase 'March comes in like a lion,' they must have been talking about coastal Maine," she said aloud. Although Maggie had lived in Vermont for many years, the weather here in Somerset Harbor, where she had inherited a mansion right on the water, was far more changeable and often ferocious.

At the word *lion*, Snickers rolled over onto his belly, lifting his head regally and blinking his eyes as though to say, "And who is king of the beasts in this house?"

"No doubt about it, you rule the roost, Snickers." With a laugh, Maggie picked up the next letter in the pile. After a long day at Carriage House Antiques, the business also bequeathed to her by her aunt Evelyn Bradbury, she was reading her mail and drinking a welcome cup of tea. Then she'd eat a light supper—already warming in the oven—before heading down to the historical society for an evening meeting.

Not that I want to go out in that, Maggie thought, shivering as the wind rattled the windows. But society president Ruth Harper and the others were counting on her to help with a new exhibit featuring Somerset Harbor during World War II. One of the last living veterans in town had a birthday in March, and Ruth had something special planned to share at the meeting.

While her pet closed his eyes in a doze, Maggie opened electric bills, a delivery invoice for heating oil, and a bank statement for the store. Spring's arrival—if it ever came—would mean lower utility bills, and for that Maggie was grateful. With Somerset Harbor's cool ocean breeze, she rarely had to use air conditioning. Open windows with screens were enough.

Movement outside caught her eye, and for a moment in the dim dusk light, she thought she saw a slump-shouldered figure trudging along the front of the house. Then she blinked and it was gone. Maybe she imagined it.

The next envelope was from Old Faith Chapel, Maggie's church. She opened it curiously, since Pastor David Young didn't ask for anything very often.

Dear Maggie,

Many people don't realize that homelessness is a problem in Maine. Here at the church, we are forced to turn people away every week. Many of these men and women are regulars at our soup kitchen. We can give them a hot meal, but then, after our few beds are full, we have to send them on their way to the nearest shelter, which is fifteen miles away. We're partnering with other area churches to expand our small shelter here in Somerset Harbor. Won't you join us in putting a roof over the heads of these vulnerable neighbors? Permanent housing assistance and other services are also planned. As Jesus said, "I was a stranger and you took Me in."

Maggie's heart twisted at the idea that homeless men and women were roaming the cold woods and fields of Maine.

How terrible. Picking up a pen, she quickly scrawled a pledge. Perhaps she could also donate some furniture. Bed frames and armchairs would probably be welcome. She'd have to ask Pastor David.

The timer chimed in the kitchen and Maggie put aside the envelopes and hoisted herself out of the cushy sofa. "Time for dinner. Coming?" Snickers leaped from his seat and bolted past her. She chuckled, amused as always at how a cat could go from dead asleep to fully alert in a split second.

After Maggie pulled a homemade chicken-and-rice casserole out of the oven to cool, she fed the cat and put on a pot of coffee. The stormy weather made her feel sleepy and she needed a shot of energy to get through the evening. If only she could figure out how Snickers did it.

An hour later, Maggie put on her rubber-soled boots and car coat, adding a pair of fleece-lined leather gloves and a wool hat. As she tugged the hat low over her ears, she made a face at herself in the hall mirror, feeling frumpy. She thought of her college-age daughter, Emily, who looked beautiful no matter what she wore but especially in hats of all styles.

Emily was going to school at St. Joseph's College in Standish, Maine, just far enough away that Maggie didn't see her often but close enough to drive. Other friends had children attending college clear across the country. Maggie's heart couldn't handle that distance, not yet. It was still a little tender from the loss of her husband, Richard, a college professor, several years before.

A light snow was now falling, tiny icy flakes blowing into Maggie's face as she crossed the driveway. She hoped there wouldn't be enough accumulation to make the trip home slippery. Although Maggie's Jetta was good in snow, she hated winter driving. As she approached her car, she saw something tucked under the windshield wiper.

The person in the driveway. *Did someone actually come up here to leave an advertisement?* She'd gotten flyers plastered on her car in parking lots but not usually here at home on Shoreline Drive, a couple of blocks from the downtown waterfront.

She picked up the wiper and plucked the piece of paper off the windshield. It was small, the size and shape of a playing card. As she turned it over, she realized it *was* a playing card—the queen of diamonds. *How very strange.*

Maggie tucked it into her pocket and opened the car door. If she didn't hurry, she was going to be late. Sliding inside, she started the engine, turned on the wipers to clear the glass, and switched the blower to high. She always did that, even if she knew full well that minutes would go by before the engine would give off heat. She would probably be at the meeting before her car was warm. It was a psychological trick to convince herself she was nice and toasty instead of braced against the cold in a frigid automobile.

One of the best things about living in Somerset Harbor was that nothing was very far from anything else. It was only a matter of minutes before Maggie turned onto Wharf Road, passed one of her favorite restaurants, The Lobster Quadrille, and found a parking spot. On this wintry evening, almost no one was out and about. When she shut her car door, she winced at how loud it sounded in the empty street. Gusting snow swirled in the streetlights, their dim glow revealing crusty snowbanks edging the sidewalks.

Maggie pulled her collar up against the drafty air and hurried across the street to her destination, a lovely rose-pink Queen Anne Victorian—complete with a turret, teal accents, and white gingerbread trim—that housed the society. Bright lights made the building glow with warmth, a cheerful sight on such a gloomy night.

After stamping her boots on the porch mat to loosen snow and ice, Maggie opened the tall oak door and stepped inside. The heat lent a flush to her chilled cheeks.

"Is that you, Maggie?" Ruth Harper called from the adjacent room.

"It is." Maggie removed her outerwear and hung her coat on a peg, joining the variety already stowed there. She recognized Ruth's navy wool, Liz Young's pink parka with its white faux-fur trim, June McGillis's belted burgundy topper, and Ina Linton's neon-green down jacket. She smiled at this last. The garment evoked her elderly friend's eccentric and lively personality. Ina claimed the coat helped make her more visible to traffic, since she walked everywhere despite being well over seventy years old. Maggie didn't doubt her assertion.

The ladies were seated around a big table, helping Ruth sort through boxes of items, examining each and selecting the best for the display. A banner across the wall read, *Somerset Harbor During World War II.*

"Take a seat, Maggie," Ruth said, gesturing to an empty chair. "We're preparing two exhibits, one featuring our soldiers and the other their loved ones at home."

Maggie slid into a seat beside Ina. A cardboard box filled with newspapers and other collectibles waited on the table in front of her.

"Glad you could make it," Ina said. "On a nasty night like this I had to force myself to leave the house."

"I'm sick of winter too," Liz said with a laugh. "This year it seems like it's dragging on forever." A counselor, Liz was also Pastor David's wife and worked with various organizations in the church. Maggie figured she'd have a big hand in the renovation of the homeless shelter.

"I hear you," Ruth said. "I had to order another tank of oil."

She adjusted her eyeglasses to better peer at a booklet titled *Wartime Saving Secrets*. She harrumphed. "Maybe I should study this."

"I bet there's a lot of good information in there," Liz said. "During World War II, almost everything was rationed. Coffee, silk stockings, food, gas."

"Not to age myself," Ina said, "but I remember my mother being thrilled whenever she got a new pair of stockings, even after rationing ended."

Maggie gently removed a stack of fragile, yellowing editions of the *Somerset Harbor Herald* and set them on the table. *U.S. Attacked!* screamed a huge headline dated December 7, 1941. The paper had issued a special edition.

She shivered, imagining the emotions of those reading the alarming news. It must have been very similar to her reaction to hearing about the 9/11 attacks—shock, horror, fear, uncertainty about the future.

"What strikes me," June said, "is how everyone pulled together." June was the manager of Carriage House Antiques and Maggie's good friend. "Look at these." She stood to display several posters urging people to save scrap metal, collect for war bonds, and grow victory gardens.

"They're wonderful," Maggie said. "I love the graphics."

"I'd like to convey that sense of patriotism in our exhibit," Ruth said. Her cheeks flushed with enthusiasm. "I want everyone to be uplifted by how our little town responded to the war effort." She pointed to several cardboard cartons next to a display case. "Those boxes were left to me by one of my aunts. She was really active with a Red Cross group that I want to feature."

"I think my mother was part of that group," Ina said. "She was a joiner and a doer."

"And no doubt a Sedgwick relative of mine was also."

Maggie thought about Evelyn's journal, the record of antiques and their stories her late aunt had kept. Maybe she had tucked away some World War II memorabilia in the storage room or the attic. "I'll see what I can find at the mansion." She opened a newspaper carefully so as not to rip the fragile paper. "And I'll look for references to the Red Cross in these papers."

"Maybe you'll find some articles with names and we'll be able to track down their family members," June suggested.

"Those were the days when even this meeting would make the papers," Ina said. "They had the social column, remember?"

"I do," Ruth said with a chuckle. "It included tea parties, out-of-town visitors, what the who's who of society was doing. How quaint."

The ladies worked quietly for a few minutes, accompanied by the howling wind and the big band songs June played for them on her portable player. "I thought these would help us get in the mood," she said.

When "Back Home for Keeps" came on, a dreamy look crossed Ina's face and she said, "I remember my mother and father dancing to that."

Maggie had always enjoyed the swooping horns and smooth melodies of the era, and she found herself singing along under her breath. Between tracks, she asked Ruth, "So tell me, what *are* we doing to celebrate our veteran's birthday?"

"Originally I thought we'd have a party here, but this house won't be big enough." Ruth grinned with satisfaction. "So I booked the town hall."

Everyone burst into cries of excitement. The nicely appointed hall, site of annual town meetings, could easily hold hundreds. It also had a service kitchen, very handy for catering events.

"We're expecting a crowd then," Ina said. "Won't that be nice for William King and his family?"

June gave a yelp of excitement, waving the cookbook she held. "I just had a great idea. We're planning to serve food, right? How about a buffet featuring dishes from the 1940s?"

Ina leafed through the book. "Gelatin salad, meat croquettes, Welsh rarebit. This is bringing back childhood memories. There's even something called home front macaroni."

"Even better, let's use recipes that take rationing into account," Liz said. She made a rueful grimace. "I think running the soup kitchen has ingrained thrifty cooking into my brain."

"The kitchen is part of the homeless initiative, right?" Maggie asked. "I got the church's letter today."

"Actually, I think the kitchen sparked that initiative," Liz said. "Another church nearby was running the program for years, but the elderly members couldn't do it anymore, so we took over both a couple of weeks ago. I have to admit, I had no idea how bad the homeless situation was."

June reached out to pat Liz's arm. "Hold that thought on the shelter. I just had another idea for our event."

"You're batting a thousand tonight, June," Ina said. "Bring it on."

"Let's do a World War II antique kitchen vignette at the town hall. We can auction off the pieces to benefit the shelter." June turned to Maggie. "I figure we can find the items through our shop contacts." Maggie and June not only bought inventory up and down the Maine coast, but they were also connected to a network of dealers. If they couldn't find something, maybe one of their colleagues could.

"I love that idea," Liz said. "Many of our homeless are veterans. The shelter will take all the funding we can get. Right now we're using the old rectory but it needs a lot of work." She turned to the society president. "Ruth, what do you think? After all, the party is a historical society event."

Ruth shrugged. "I don't have a problem with raising money for the shelter." She paused, then grinned. "Because the fashion show will benefit this place."

Once again, the others reacted with enthusiasm. Maggie thought about the racks of vintage clothing she'd seen in the second-floor storeroom at the manor. "I think I have some 1940s outfits at home."

"And we know several clothing dealers too," June said. "I'll get on it tomorrow."

"I guess this is a good time to show you what I brought." Ruth got up and grabbed the largest of her cardboard boxes. Despite its size, it appeared light, because she easily moved it to the table. She pulled open the flaps. "I don't know if I told you this, but my mom's sister, my aunt Lillian, was a milliner." The first object she removed was a framed photograph that depicted a pretty blonde woman sporting a newsboy hat.

"You mean a hatmaker?" Ina asked. "Now there's a profession that has gone the way of the dodo bird."

"Aunt Lillian lived on the outskirts of Somerset Harbor, on the Spade family farm, so she sold her hats at shops in town. Or by special order." Ruth gently pulled out a tissue-wrapped object, pulling away the paper to reveal a black velvet cartwheel hat trimmed with white roses. She handed it to June. "Try it on."

Ruth gave Liz a navy blue straw topper that perched fetchingly over her brow, and Ina a silk turban with a jewel and feather. She handed Maggie a black velvet style that clung to the head, red berries dangling jauntily on one side. "That's called a capulet," Ruth said. She put a gray pillbox trimmed with pink flowers on her own head.

"Black velvet must have been popular back then," Maggie said. She carried the hat to a mirror to settle it on her head properly. Something in the hatband didn't lie flat so she pulled the hat off to see what it was.

A piece of paper was tucked underneath the ribbon. "I've found something," she called to the others. She teased it out with her fingers and unfolded it.

A letter, handwritten in German.

"What is it, Maggie?" June asked.

Maggie started, realizing she'd been staring at the piece of paper. "It's a letter." She squinted, recognizing the word *Lillian*. She handed it to Ruth. "Addressed to your aunt."

Ruth took the paper, her forehead wrinkled in confusion. "I see her name, but the rest of it is in . . . German? Why would someone write my aunt a note in German?"

"Did she have any friends in Germany?" Liz asked. "Maybe the solution is simple. I had a French pen pal back in high school. She wrote to me in French and I wrote back in English."

"I don't think this is a pen pal message," Ruth said. "Listen to the date." She sounded out the words, "'25, *März 1943*.' March 25th, 1943." Her hands shook. "What does this mean? She was a very patriotic woman. The top collector of war bonds on this part of the Maine coast." Ruth sank into a chair, obviously overcome.

"There were German prisoner-of-war camps in Maine," June said. "I remember attending a presentation about them. They sent prisoners all over the country. Maybe she had something to do with one of the camps."

Ruth shook her head. "Prisoners of war? Surely a story like that would have come down through the family."

"Let me find out what it says," Maggie said. "I'll text it to Emily and ask her if there is a professor at the college willing to translate for us." She snapped a photo of the note with her phone, then sent it to her daughter with a message saying she'd tell her more about it later.

Just then, the front door of the museum opened with a rattle of the doorknob, and Maggie heard the rumble of a man talking.

Ruth jumped to her feet. "Our guests are here." She thrust the paper at Maggie, who tucked it into the pocket of her corduroys. "Please do send it to Emily." Her mouth turned down. "I'll keep my fingers crossed that it's innocent." With a shudder, she straightened her skirt and squared her shoulders. June turned down the music a little.

Two men entered the main room, the older one tall and very thin with white hair in a crest, the other shorter and stout, holding the other by the arm. "Come on, Dad. Don't trip on the threshold."

Although they were related, Maggie thought they couldn't be more different in demeanor as well as appearance. The veteran William King appeared gentle and rather vague as his pale blue eyes rested on each woman in turn. In contrast, his son wore a perpetual scowl, his thick brows almost meeting over an assertive nose. He didn't make eye contact as he guided his father to a chair between Ina and June.

"I don't want him to fall and break his hip," the son said. "Women aren't the only ones who suffer from osteoporosis, you know." His tone was aggrieved, almost challenging.

"We do now," Ina said. At Ruth's quelling glance, she added, "I'm sorry to hear that." She patted William's hand in sympathy.

"Who are you?" William asked. "You remind me of someone."

"I'm Ina Linton. Maybe you remember my mother, Doris."

William plucked at his lip. "Doris, hmm. I used to know a Doris." A look of confusion passed over his face. "I think."

His son made a dismissive sound. "He doesn't remember anything unless it has to do with World War II." He crossed his arms and gazed at Ruth expectantly.

"I'm sorry. Where are my manners? Let me introduce you." Ruth addressed the room. "Everybody, this is William King and his son, Ronald King. Ronald is sponsoring the birthday party." Everyone responded with exclamations of gratitude and appreciation.

Ronald's plump cheeks flushed as he preened. "Hey, it's the least I can do for the old fellow. He's one of the few World War II veterans left in Somerset Harbor, and I think it's important we acknowledge that." He laughed, revealing large square teeth. "Now that we've met, can I ask you all something? What in tarnation are you wearing on your heads?" He pulled back a chair and sat beside his father.

Maggie looked around and realized that the others still wore Lillian's creations.

Ruth reached up and gently removed the gray pillbox from her head. "These are hats from the World War II era. My aunt made them." She set hers on the counter and the others followed suit, making a line of lovely hats. Then they joined the Kings at the table.

"Let's talk about the party," Ronald said. His lip curled. "This room is nice, but it's way too small." He peered from corner to corner. "You couldn't swing a cat in here."

"You're right, Ronald," Ruth said. "That's why I've booked the town hall."

Ronald pulled his head back in surprise. "What's that like?"

"You don't know?" Ina asked. "That's right, you're a newcomer." She gave her trademark cackle. "Welcome to Somerset Harbor." With Ina, that greeting might be a promise or a warning, depending on what she thought of someone.

"Er, thanks." Ronald's tone was doubtful. "My dad grew up here, but I was born and raised in Bangor, where he moved after the war."

William, who had been studying his hands intently, roused himself to say, "Ray was born there too."

"That's right, Ray was born in Bangor." Ronald gave him a dismissive pat on the arm.

Who is Ray? William, who was daydreaming again, apparently wasn't going to enlighten them. Maggie felt a pang of sympathy for the poor man, who seemed to be suffering from some kind of dementia.

"Anyway, once I sold my stores, I decided to retire to Somerset Harbor and bring Dad back to his old stomping grounds."

Poor old William won't be doing much stomping. Maggie resolved to help make his birthday the party of a lifetime.

"So, back to the town hall," Ruth said. "It can hold hundreds. Plus, I thought we could get a banner to drape across the main entrance wishing William a happy birthday. We'll make it a town-wide celebration."

Ronald rubbed his chin. "I like that. I want Dad to get the recognition he deserves." He lowered his voice to speak behind his hand. "Even if he doesn't know what's going on half the time."

Maggie was stunned at the man's rudeness but she had to bite back a laugh when William said, "Be careful there, sonny. I know more than you think."

Ronald flushed a deep, ugly red, but he covered his embarrassment by throwing back his head and guffawing. "That's Dad for you—always a kidder."

Ruth gave a pressed-lip smile. "Anyway, we're planning a buffet meal, a fashion show, and an auction, all with a '40s theme."

"Really? All that? It *will* be quite an event." Ronald sounded impressed.

"Let's dance," William said. "I used to be quite the hoofer." He swayed to the soft strains of "Sentimental Journey." Maggie had forgotten that June's portable record player was still providing background music.

"We can do that," Ruth said. "Dancing would be fun. Maybe after the auction."

"Daisy and her husband used to be in a swing dance group," June said. "Maybe they'll be willing to give lessons at the party." She explained to Ronald that Daisy Carter owned The Busy Bean café on the waterfront and her husband, Harry, was a lobsterman.

"Oh yes, the Bean. I go there a lot. My grandson loves the hot chocolate."

"So do I," Ina said with a smack of her lips. "Daisy really piles on the whipped cream."

"I think a dance is a great idea," Liz said. "David and I have done ballroom dancing but not swing." She grimaced. "I hope our hips and knees can take it."

Maggie pictured the lively movements of the Lindy Hop and had to concur. She couldn't imagine someone picking her up and tossing her around. "The young people will like it even if us old folks sit out." Maybe Emily and her friends could come.

"Daisy won't let you sit," Ina said with a laugh. "I've been around her when she's doing her thing."

As the conversation transpired, William's gaze wandered around the room and rested briefly on a mannequin wearing an Army uniform with a hard hat. He pushed back his chair and stood, tottering over to take a close look. "I used to wear something like this."

"Dad was in the 10th Mountain Division," Ronald said. "He fought in Italy."

"Those are the men who used skis, right?" Ina asked.

"Correct. They had to traverse the Italian mountains on foot so they mountain-climbed or skied. I think we still have his white ski uniform. I can bring it over, if you want."

"We'd love it," Ruth said. "Thanks so much for your generosity."

William was now looking at the hats. Then he picked up the picture of Lillian and studied her pretty face, his own breaking out into a huge smile. "This is Lillian Spade. I remember Lillian. I was in love with her." He chuckled. "Even if she was five years older than me."

Ruth's brows rose. "Really? I love to hear stories about my relatives. What else do you remember?" She sent Maggie a significant glance, and Maggie knew they were thinking the same thing: Maybe William knew the origin of the German note.

William clutched the picture in both hands, his expression dreamy. "I remember her golden hair, how it used to gleam in the firelight. She had the most delicate hands. I used to watch her make hats. She'd take a bunch of nothing and whip up something beautiful." A frown creased his brow. "It's not true what they said about her."

Ronald shifted in his chair, seeming once again to be embarrassed by his father. "Dad, let's not talk about Lillian." He glanced at his gold watch. "It's time for us to go." With a stretch of his arms, he got up and went to join his father. He took the photograph out of William's unresisting hands. "Let's go see Chris and Trevor. They're waiting for us at home."

William allowed Ronald to steer him away from the counter and toward the door.

"We'll be in touch," Ronald called over his shoulder. "Thanks again for everything."

After some mumbling in the hall, where Ronald helped William with his coat and hat, the door slammed behind them. A moment later, the door opened again.

"Did they forget something?" Ruth half rose.

Then a familiar voice with a Southern twang was heard. "*Brr.* It's freezing out there. You'd think after thirty years I'd be used to it."

"Daisy!" Maggie said with a smile. Their friend was a transplant from the South, and while she loved Maine, her personality and appearance still had a Southern belle flair.

The former beauty queen appeared in the doorway, followed by Fran Vosburg, the youngest member of the group, and Deborah Bennett, mother of alderman James Bennett.

"Sorry we're late." Fran's cheeks were pink with cold. "Daisy and I stopped by Deborah's to pick her up. Look what she brought."

Deborah held up a black photograph album with both hands, smiling widely. "My mother-in-law's photos. She was very active in Somerset Harbor's war efforts."

"Perfect," Ruth said. "Grab some coffee and come sit down. We've made a lot of progress."

"Did you assign us chores?" Daisy asked with a laugh. "My aunt always said that latecomers get the worst assignments. That was her way of encouraging us to be on time."

"Nothing like that," Liz said. "But we've decided to include a fashion show, 1940s buffet, swing dancing, and an auction at the birthday party."

"Is that all?" Deborah gave one of her sweet smiles. "Surely we can do better than that."

Everyone laughed. "Was that Ronald King I saw walking to his car?" Daisy asked. At Ruth's nod, she added, "What'd he think of our plans?"

Ruth exchanged glances with the others. "He seemed to like them okay. He's really happy about having his father honored."

"I take it he was the older gentleman with Ronald?" Fran asked. "I've seen him around town. He's a bit muddled, but nice."

June took a sip of her coffee. "The poor man seems to be more aware of the past than what's going on now."

"I noticed that too," Liz said. "He certainly perked up when he saw the picture of Ruth's aunt Lillian, though." She pointed to the photograph on the counter. "Apparently he knew her."

"She was a hatmaker, right?" Fran asked. "I take it these are her work." She picked up the capulet and set it on her head.

"Maggie found a note inside that hat," Ina said. "In German."

Fran whirled around, almost losing the hat. She had to reach up and hold it in place. "That's strange."

"I thought so too," Ruth said. "In fact it's quite upsetting. I can't figure out how my aunt would have known anyone German during the war. The note is dated 1943, you see."

"Can I take a look?" Daisy asked. Maggie passed her the message. She sucked in a breath. "I sure wish I could translate it for you." Daisy gave the note to Fran and Deborah, who both scanned it and shook their heads.

"Don't worry, we'll help you figure it out, Ruth," June said.

Daisy added, "I'm sure your aunt was innocent of any wrongdoing."

"I hope you're right," Ruth said. She sighed. "But let's get back to the exhibit. Which of those hats do you think we should display?"

"All of them," Maggie and Fran said in unison. The group laughed again.

"We'll do that if I can find enough mannequin heads," Ruth said. "Or hat stands."

"I'll help with that," June said. "I have some calls I can make."

"This exhibit is really shaping up," Fran said. "I have a vintage victory quilt made from feed sacks to contribute. A woman brought it in the other day for me to appraise and I couldn't resist—I bought it." Fran owned The Quilt Cupboard, a shop located across from The Busy Bean.

They browsed through Ruth's artifacts quietly for a while, setting aside the most interesting items. While she leafed through antique postcard views of Somerset Harbor and the surrounding area, Maggie thought back to Ronald and William's visit. "William mentioned someone named Ray, born in Bangor the same as Ronald. Does that ring a bell for anyone? I'm just curious."

Daisy, who was leafing through old letters and telegrams, lifted her head. "Oh, sweet pea, there's another mystery for you. Ray King is Ronald's brother. And he disappeared years ago."

3

Gasps flew around the circle. Daisy tipped her head, considering. "Actually, he disappeared twice. But the second time is the real mystery."

Ina bounced in her seat. "Go on, Daisy. Spill it." Ina loved mysteries—and solving them.

"Let me start at the beginning." Someone groaned. Daisy held up a hand. "It's not a long story, promise." She paused to build tension, one of her habits. "Ray King is William King's younger son. The family lived in Bangor when tragedy struck. At the time, Ray was married to a woman named Laurie, and they had an eight-year-old son, Chris."

"But Chris is the name of Ronald's son," Liz protested.

"I know. This is where it gets strange. First you need to know this. Ray was a brilliant man, but subject to depression, I've gathered. He did successfully serve in the military and was going to medical school after getting out. But during an ice storm in March over twenty years ago, there was a terrible car accident. Laurie was thrown from the car and killed. In addition to suffering terrible injuries, Ray had a breakdown and was sent to a private hospital, only no one knew that. The police never pressed charges for his role in the accident."

"The first disappearance," Ruth said. "The family swept it all under the rug?"

"From what I've heard, yes. That was common back then. Ronald stepped forward and adopted Chris as his own. According to my sources, Ray was never mentioned again."

"It was nice of Ronald to adopt Chris, give him a family,"

Deborah said. She herself had been raised by her mother and an aunt.

"Except he still had a father," Daisy said. "Even if he was a patient at Avalon Hospital."

"I've heard of that place," Fran said. "It's a pretty swanky private facility."

"What happened to Ray?" Maggie asked. She had the feeling it couldn't be good.

Daisy shrugged. "When they released him, apparently he vanished."

"And no one knows where he is?" Ruth frowned. "That's awful."

"If they do, they aren't saying," Daisy said. "Now keep in mind this was shared with me by some old-timers down at the café. The accident was big news around here because William was a Somerset Harbor native. The rest is fill-in-the-blanks from someone's sister in Bangor, etcetera. You know the drill."

"The outcome all depends on follow-up care," Liz said. "Many formerly hospitalized adults become homeless if they don't have the right support. A number of the men and women who sleep at our shelter are mentally ill or disabled."

Maggie's heart went out to these unfortunates. "Liz, I'm so glad you're trying to add beds to the shelter. I can't stand the thought of those poor souls wandering around without help." The others echoed her sentiments.

Liz smiled at her friends. "We can always use volunteers at the soup kitchen. You're welcome to come tomorrow night. Yes, these folks need a helping hand, but they have a lot to offer. I'm always the one who feels blessed."

The meeting broke up soon after and Maggie drove home through the frigid night, shivering all the way. With a feeling of gratitude, she pulled up in front of the house and dashed to unlock the door. The gust of warm air and the meowing cat that greeted her were both welcome.

She bent to pet Snickers. "How about a bedtime snack?" She wasn't hungry, but a hot drink sounded heavenly. After giving the kitty a few treats, she filled the kettle for herbal tea. Then she sat in the breakfast nook to check her e-mails on her laptop. One was a note from Emily telling her she'd gotten the photo of Lillian's note Maggie had texted her. Emily's e-mail was brief, of course, but she appreciated it all the same. For a moment, she pictured her lively daughter, probably in the library or her dorm room at this hour, laughing and chatting with friends over their books and notes. Smiling, Maggie wrote her back, asking if Emily could find someone to translate it.

The kettle whistled, so Maggie made her tea and kept browsing. Ray's tragic story kept circling around in her mind. Maybe the Bangor newspaper archive had something.

She was in luck. *Bangor Woman Killed in Late-Night Accident.* The story detailed the event, which happened during an ice storm. Laurie King died instantly when the family sedan collided with another vehicle and she was thrown from the car. Bleeding from a head wound, Ray was found wandering around nearby, disoriented, while their son, who had sustained his own head injury, was unconscious in the back seat. A photograph accompanied the story. Maggie peered at it with a sick feeling in her belly. Oddly, the back door as well as the driver's-side door was open. Had Ray checked on the boy in his confused state?

She read on. The other driver, a Stewart Gates, was also seriously injured. The police were investigating the cause of the accident, citing icy roads as a contributing factor.

Maggie, who had enjoyed a long and happy marriage until her husband's untimely death, could barely fathom Ray's state of mind. How terrible that he had been the one driving when his wife died! How could he ever recover from something like that?

Picking up her mug, Maggie clasped it in both hands, savoring the comforting warmth. She realized she was sitting with her shoulders hunched forward as though cradling herself against Ray King's distressing story. Taking a deep breath, she forced herself to relax. She couldn't solve all the world's problems, but she could try to make life a little better for the people around her.

She'd go to the soup kitchen and volunteer, she decided. It was the least she could do.

• • • • • • • • • • • • • • • •

The weather was slightly warmer the next morning, so Maggie enjoyed her walk over to the shop. The path led through woods, and the bridge crossing a stream was one of her favorite places to stop for a minute. With pleasure, Maggie inhaled crisp air scented with the very beginnings of spring. In every season, the spot was peaceful and serene, if ever-changing. Today the stream gurgled below the thin sheet of ice connected to the rocks, and bare patches under trees revealed deep green moss. Soon new ferns and other woodland plants would emerge, and tender green leaves would cover the undergrowth and trees.

At peace with her world, Maggie set off toward the store with a spring in her step. The sight of James Bennett's truck out front gave her an extra boost. The handsome alderman was also a historical preservation consultant who did some hands-on restoration of antiques and buildings. She was glad he'd finally gotten a truck for when he had to haul antique furniture, especially in this weather.

"Good morning, Maggie." June's chipper voice greeted her as she entered the shop.

Maggie glanced around but couldn't see her manager anywhere. "Umm, where are you?"

June popped up from behind a chubby armchair upholstered in flocked burgundy. "Hi. James and I are looking at the wiring in this radio."

Next to the chair stood a cabinet radio. As Maggie moved closer, she saw James kneeling behind it. "Get someone to put in new tubes and check the wiring," he said. "Other than that, it looks to be in good condition."

"I take it this is the newest vignette," Maggie said. June set up different room-like settings quite often, reflecting the season or special events. This one appeared to be a 1940s living room, complete with doilies on the furniture arms and a copy of *Life* magazine on the coffee table. A china cabinet held Depression glass and lusterware.

June nodded enthusiastically. "I was inspired by our meeting last night. I have to admit, the World War II era fascinates me."

"Me too," James said. "I'm kind of a buff. An uncle left me a whole collection of books on the battles. I also like the documentaries on television."

"Coffee, you two?" At their nods, June went into the back room to brew a pot.

"William King was in the 10th Mountain Division," Maggie said. "Do you know much about them?"

James's eyes lit up. "Oh yes. They did all kinds of interesting missions overseas. Men from New England who could ski or mountaineer were popular on their list of recruits. Many went on to found ski areas after the war."

"That's an interesting bit of information. I don't know what William did after the war." Maggie wandered over to the counter, where she perched on a stool.

"I think he became a doctor," James said. "But his father and grandfather were carpenters here in Somerset Harbor. I've come across quite a few houses built by them in my renovation work."

June bustled out of the back with a tray of mugs. "Ronald owned stores, he said."

James took a mug and added cream. "A string of pharmacies. They were bought out by one of the bigger chains. I remember their ads. 'King's Drugstores—where you're treated like royalty.'"

Maggie sipped her coffee, enjoying the camaraderie of her colleagues. One of the most interesting parts of running an antiques business was the backstory, both behind individual pieces and the time periods they came from. *It's all about the stories.*

"Meeting William and Ronald wasn't the only interesting thing that happened at the meeting last night," Maggie said to James. "We all tried on 1940s hats made by Ruth's aunt Lillian. Would you believe I found a note written in German in mine dated 1943?"

James spluttered, almost spitting out his coffee. He wiped his mouth. "A note from 1943 written in German?"

"Crazy, right?" June said. "Ruth had no idea how it got there."

"If there's a mystery, trust Maggie to find it." His eyes twinkled with good humor.

"I guess I'm a mystery magnet." Maggie set her mug down. "That reminds me. I'm going to text Emily and see if she found anyone who can translate that message." She pulled out her phone and sent the message.

While she was doing that, June filled James in about the party plans. "I heard Ruth was booking the hall," James said, "but I didn't realize the scope of the event. Wow."

"We came up with the rest of the plans at our meeting last night," June said. "And that reminds me, I'll start checking around for World War II kitchen items today for our auction."

"I know a man who restores old gas stoves and refrigerators," James said. "They're gorgeous." He leafed through his phone and showed Maggie and June photos from the website. Maggie's favorite stove was pale green and cream with legs. She also liked a round-top refrigerator that resembled one her grandmother had owned.

"I'll give him a call too," June said. "Send me the link."

"If you need me to pick anything up, let me know," James said. "We can use my new truck."

"What a nice offer," Maggie said. "We'll take you up on that, I'm sure."

"Please do." James emptied his cup. "Thanks for the coffee. I hate to say this but I've got to get going. Client appointment." He moved toward the coatrack.

"If you're not doing anything tonight, come by the soup kitchen," Maggie called. "I'm going to be volunteering."

Coat half-on, James paused. "Really? Maybe I will." He shrugged it the rest of the way on. "Nice way to give back, right?"

When the door closed behind him, Maggie made a point of not looking at June, who was smirking.

. . . .

As dusk was falling late that afternoon, Maggie parked behind the church, recognizing a few of the cars already there as belonging to Ruth, Daisy, and Fran. A good turnout of volunteers then. Old Faith Chapel's parish hall was in the back, behind the sanctuary and offices.

Lights gleamed in the building, beckoning to her as she picked her way across the icy, rutted parking lot. If the parish hall seemed a sanctuary to her, how must it feel to the homeless men and women who would soon arrive?

Inside the back door was a small hall with coatracks. After hanging up her jacket, Maggie took off her boots and slipped on the shoes she'd brought with her. Straight ahead was the hall, set up with long tables and chairs. Through an open pass-through to the kitchen, Maggie glimpsed people moving about. She hurried to join them.

"Hi, everyone," she called as she entered the kitchen. The others looked up and greeted her. Liz and Fran were at a table putting together big bowls of salad while Ina and Ruth were monitoring large vats of boiling water and sauce. Daisy was at the other oven checking on a pan of baking meatballs.

"What can I do?" Maggie asked.

"How about making the garlic bread?" Liz suggested. She showed Maggie a half dozen long loaves of bread donated by a grocery store. "Slice these open, butter them, and sprinkle on garlic powder. Then wrap them in foil."

Maggie washed her hands, then opened the first loaf. By the amount of food they were making, she guessed they would be feeding about fifty people. *There can't be that many living on the street! Not in Somerset Harbor. Can there?* "Is everyone who comes to the dinner homeless?" she murmured to Liz.

Liz shook her head. "No, it's a community dinner, open to all. We get the elderly, those trying to make ends meet, and some who just don't want to eat alone." Her brow creased. "But for our homeless, this is one of the few meals they can count on."

Maggie made regular slices along the top of the loaf. "Was all this food donated?"

"Yes, the grocery stores take turns," Liz said. "We use cash donations to fill in what isn't given to us." She patted Maggie on the shoulder. "I'm going to get back to the salads."

The group of women worked companionably to prepare the meal. Guests drifted into the main room, sitting and visiting while enjoying the hot coffee and tea provided. One man broke out a guitar and strummed softly, playing nice background music. Pastor David and other volunteers, including a newly arrived James, set the tables. Maggie noticed Ronald King had shown up,

Ronald reached Trevor's side first. "What did he give you?" Snatching the card from the child's hand, he stared toward the doorway. But Ace was gone, out into the cold night.

Liz and Maggie, seated nearby, joined Ronald. The card was an ace of hearts, Maggie noticed. She thought of the card she'd found on her car, the queen of diamonds. *Did Ace leave it for me to thank me for the money I'd given him? It's possible.* "Do you think he was trying to say something?" Maggie asked.

"I don't like strange men talking to my grandson," Ronald huffed.

"He didn't talk to him," Liz pointed out. "And Ace is a gentle soul."

"It's all right, Dad," Chris, Ronald's son, said. "No harm done."

Trevor tugged on his grandfather's sleeve. "Can I have the card?" Dark-haired and slight, with big brown eyes, he had a charming sprinkle of freckles on his upturned nose.

Ronald reluctantly handed him the ace and Trevor clutched it, studying it closely. Maggie had the sense that, like most children, he was fascinated by anything out of the ordinary. Receiving a gift from a mysterious homeless man had to be in that category.

His grandfather was still sputtering about the impropriety of it all, so Little Johnny picked up his guitar again and strummed. Once Little Johnny had everyone's attention, he said, "Have you all heard the song 'The Deck of Cards'? It's about a soldier in trouble for playing cards in church." He began to perform the song, more of a spoken monologue that related the symbols on playing cards to the Bible. The ace represented God, the four suits the four books of the Gospel, and a three card the Trinity. The queen represented Mary.

Even Ronald appeared mollified by the words of the song, which made the point that to the enlisted man, playing cards were reminders of Bible truths. *Ace likes to communicate in quite a similar way,* Maggie realized, *even if his meanings aren't biblical.*

Maggie leaned close to Liz and whispered, "Where do you think Ace is now?"

Liz shook her head. "I have no idea. Our beds are full tonight." She gestured at the group of homeless men and one woman seated nearby. "You can see why we want to create a larger shelter. A Maine winter is no time to camp out."

Once again, Maggie's heart filled with anguish at the thought of these poor people sleeping out in the cold. "I'm happy to contribute," Maggie said. "Personally as well as what the shop will give through the auction. June and I agreed that we'll donate any of the 1940s furniture we acquire."

"I'm so glad to hear that," Liz said. "I can't tell you enough how grateful I am for the support everyone is offering." She took a deep breath and then said, "It's a passion project for me, I don't mind telling you. An uncle of mine died homeless, in New York City."

Maggie reached out and took Liz's hand. "I'm so sorry. I had no idea."

Liz pulled out a tissue and wiped her eyes. "He had serious issues. The family tried to help but then he disappeared. A year later we got the terrible news." She lowered her voice to a whisper. "He died of pneumonia."

"Oh, Liz, I'm so sorry," Maggie said again. In the face of such a tragedy, her words felt inadequate.

Pastor David came up to the table and put a hand on his wife's shoulder. "The men are going to start cleaning up. You ladies can go home and rest. It's our turn to work."

"Thanks, dear." At the sight of her husband, Liz's sorrowful expression disappeared, replaced by a twinkling smile. She pushed back her chair and got up, followed by Maggie and the other women. People milled around, chattering, making to-go bags, and putting on their coats to leave. A couple of men started clearing while others began folding chairs.

James came over to Maggie as she was putting on her coat. "Glad to see you made it," Maggie said.

"I'm happy I did. A nice group of folks." James grinned. "Delicious meal too."

"I agree. Daisy's meatballs were spectacular." Maggie stepped out of her shoes. "And wasn't the garlic bread good?" She winked.

"Sure was." James hovered as she slipped on her boots. "I wanted to tell you, I might have a lead on an original Hoosier cabinet for the auction. The owner said it's in perfect shape; they just don't have room for it."

"That would be wonderful." Hoosier cabinets were a style of kitchen furnishing built in the early twentieth century by the Hoosier Manufacturing Co. and other companies. In addition to storage shelves and compartments, they often came with canisters, spice jars, flour sifters, and sugar bins with funnels. They were fully functional kitchen pieces—not to mention popular collectibles.

"I'll keep you posted. Have a good night." With a nod goodbye, James turned to join the others working in the hall.

Maggie slipped outside, shivering as an icy wind chilled her cheeks and nipped her ears. Diamond stars twinkled in the inky sky, the clouds long gone, leaving arctic air in their place.

Across the parking lot, shadows moved under a cluster of pine trees.

Was a person standing there or was it a trick of the shifting light? Maggie peered into the dark, straining her eyes, but she couldn't see anyone. With the uneasy, prickling sense of being watched, she unlocked her car and hastily jumped inside. She must be imagining things. No one could possibly be out there in this bitter cold.

Then a car parked on the street roared to life, headlights flaring on and shining in Maggie's face. The driver pulled out and raced away.

Someone had been watching her. But who?

· · · · · · · · · · · · · · · · · ·

Emily called the next morning while Maggie was eating toast slathered in homemade peach jam for breakfast. Snickers sat beside her in the nook, hoping she'd accidentally drop something for him to enjoy.

"Hi, Mom. Nice day, huh?" Emily laughed.

Maggie glanced out the big windows, noticing the skies were overcast again. "It seems like winter is never going to end."

"I hear you. I'm dying for hot weather and sunshine. It's so gloomy out there." Emily paused. "I might have a chance to go to Florida for spring break." She had a week off from college later in the month.

"I say take it. Maybe I'll tag along." This last was met with groans, as she expected. Maggie chuckled.

"I'm mostly calling about the German note. I'm having one of the German lit professors translate it for me. Where did you find it?"

"It was the strangest thing. I was trying on a hat from the 1940s and it was inside the hatband. The hat was made by Ruth's aunt Lillian." Maggie picked up a piece of buttered wheat toast and took a bite, Snickers watching closely. Relenting, she fed him a crumb.

Curiosity sharpened Emily's voice. "The 1940s? You think it has to do with World War II?"

"Maybe. Of course, poor Ruth was upset. She couldn't believe her patriotic aunt had anything to do with Germans back then."

"I don't blame her. Why were you guys looking at 1940s hats anyway?"

Maggie explained about the exhibit and the birthday party for William King, along with the other festivities they were planning. "Maybe you and your friends could be in our fashion show. I'm going up to the storage room to look for clothes later."

"Ooh, the storage room. I love that place. Actually, the whole thing sounds fun." Emily was silent for a minute. "I'm studying world history this semester and right now we're covering World War II. Do you think Gina and I could interview William for a class assignment we're doing?" Gina was one of Emily's good friends at college, and they shared several classes.

"I can ask his son for you. William sort of comes and goes cognitively. I'll have to see if Ronald thinks he's up to it."

"Oh, poor man. I hope he can do it. It's important to get those stories down before all the veterans are gone."

Emily's interest and insight impressed Maggie, and pride bloomed in her chest that her daughter recognized the importance of preserving history. Although she would always cherish the days when Emily was an adorable little girl, she was enjoying her as a maturing adult too. "That's a really good point, Em. He's one of the last World War II vets alive in Somerset Harbor."

"Wow. No matter what happens with the interview, I'll come help with his party, okay? What was the date again?"

Maggie told her, and it was fortunately two weeks before her break started. Emily yelped. "Sorry, Mom, got to go. I'm going to be late. My class is all the way across campus and it's freezing out there." Emily made an exaggerated shivering sound and hung up with a giggle.

As she finished her toast, Maggie found herself smiling. Yes, during these dreary, long, cold days, she wouldn't mind living somewhere warm. Many of her old friends from Vermont were snowbirds, part-time residents of both the South and New England. But Maggie was content living close to her daughter. "Nothing is more important, right, Snickers?" She reached out and stroked his head. "Including you. I wouldn't want an alligator to eat you for lunch."

He seemed to enjoy the caress, but his eyes never left her empty plate. "All right, greedy boy. I'll give you some more food." She'd noticed that he ate more in cold weather, and when her pants cut into her waistline as she bent over to fill his dish, she realized that she did too. Despite the nasty temperatures, she knew she'd better get back to her walking routine. James, who jogged along Shoreline Drive every day except during blizzards and hurricanes, was putting her to shame.

After cleaning up the breakfast dishes, Maggie went to the office and settled in behind the flame mahogany partner's desk. Her aunt had done her work here and Maggie hadn't changed a thing. The tiger oak file cabinet still held business records. Reference books lined the shelves, and, most important, a drawer in the desk held Evelyn's journal.

Maggie pulled the journal out of a drawer and began to leaf through the pages. Evelyn had not only kept a record of purchases in there, but she'd written about the story behind each piece. To Maggie's delight, she'd discovered a section that inventoried the contents of the manor, including the second-floor storage room. That room was packed to the gills with all kinds of treasures.

She searched for references to the 1940s and found notes on Barbara Sedgwick, chatelaine of the mansion at that time. According to Evelyn, in addition to being a skilled seamstress who made her own clothes, many of which were stored upstairs,

Barbara was very active in the community. She'd led metal drives, rolled bandages, and sold bonds during the war, while her husband, Captain Andrew Sedgwick, was overseas serving as a bomber pilot.

This last made Maggie's pulse leap. Barbara must have known Lillian, then. Somerset Harbor was small, after all, not much more than a village. Maggie turned the page, hoping to read more.

A yellowed, brittle clipping was tucked into the journal. Careful not to tear it, she pulled it out and unfolded it. It was a headline from Somerset Harbor's newspaper, the *Herald*, dated March 16, 1943.

German Spies Land on Maine Coast. Manhunt Under Way.

5

German spies landed in Maine? Maggie knew that U-boats had prowled the coastline and German prisoners of war were detained in the state, but never had she heard about this.

With a shiver of dismay, she read how two men had landed on a beach north of Somerset Harbor during a snowstorm. Several residents who happened to be out that night spotted the strangers. When a U-boat sank a freighter carrying sugar and molasses from the Caribbean the next day, FBI agents were soon on the trail. Residents all the way from Bangor to Boston were warned about the two spies, described as wearing topcoats and carrying suitcases.

Maggie took the clipping to the printer and made a copy, planning to show Ruth and the other members of the historical society. This was certainly a clue, even though it raised more questions than it answered.

Her cell phone rang and she hurriedly pulled it from her pocket to see who it was. James. "Good morning," she said, her heart lifting.

"And good morning to you, Maggie." James sounded excited. "I'm calling to see if you want to take a ride. We've got a deal regarding the Hoosier cabinet."

Maggie was impressed by his quick work. "Already? We just discussed that last night."

"It happened to work out," James said modestly. "When I spoke to the client this morning, I mentioned that I had someone who wanted it. So she agreed to let you look at it today, if you can."

Maggie checked her calendar. "I'm free until this afternoon, so yes."

"Let's meet at the Bean in half an hour. I thought we could have coffee first."

Daisy's café was one of Maggie's favorite places, so she readily agreed to that plan. After they hung up, she glanced down at her old, paint-spotted sweatshirt and jeans. *Uh, no.* What worked around the house wasn't really suitable for an outing with James. She really should put on something nicer.

The weather was slightly warmer today, so she chose a fisherman knit sweater, down vest, nice jeans, and duck boots, perfect for traveling on foot. She'd considered driving, but thinking of her resolution, she decided a walk was in order.

The air was brisk, with a sneaky wind that crept into any clothing gaps. She tugged her wool hat lower on her head, then balled her hands into fists and walked faster. Maybe she'd generate enough heat that way.

At any time of year, she enjoyed strolling along Shoreline Drive, with its magnificent houses and view of the water. Soon she reached the downtown section of Somerset Harbor, with its docks and wharves on one side and lines of brick and clapboard storefronts on the other. The Busy Bean was near the docks, and across the street was The Quilt Cupboard, Fran's shop. Maggie was gratified to spot a couple of women entering the store. Fran sold finished items as well as supplies, and word about her business appeared to be spreading.

Her nose practically frozen, Maggie pushed inside the warm café, the bells over the door jingling. Inside, the place was in the usual state of controlled mayhem, with customers lined up at the counter and most of the tables filled. James was waiting at Maggie's favorite table near the window.

Daisy hailed her from behind the counter. "Well hello, sunshine. How are you today?"

Maggie ran fingers through her hair, hoping it didn't look

too terrible. "Just great, thanks. I'm meeting James."

The café owner dropped her voice dramatically. "So I heard. I'll be right over with your coffee. We've got Georgia pecan today." Daisy had her own special blends made by a local roasting company.

"I'll take that. Thanks, Daisy." Maggie made her way through the tables.

James was eating an egg sandwich—Daisy's cook, Jack, made the best ones Maggie had ever tasted—while perusing the local newspaper. He put his food down when he spotted her. "Hope you don't mind I started without you. I was starving after my run."

Maggie pulled out a chair and sat. "Of course not. I already had breakfast."

Daisy brought Maggie a mug of coffee and refilled James's cup. "So what are you two up to?"

"We're going out to see a client of mine," James said. "She has a Hoosier cabinet Maggie is looking at for the benefit auction."

"And where is this client?" Daisy batted big innocent eyes framed by plenty of mascara but Maggie caught the subtext. She was hoping they were taking a long trip together.

"Out at the old Spade farm. She just bought it." James added cream to his cup and gave it a stir.

A bolt of excitement shot through Maggie, making her sit up straight. "Lillian Spade's farm?"

"I think so," James said. "She got married and left town in the 1940s so a distant branch of the family moved in. The last family member, who was quite elderly, died in December."

Who had Lillian married? Not the German spy? For a wild moment, Maggie pictured Lillian eloping with the mysterious stranger, changing their names of course. The realization that Ruth would probably know if this had happened brought her down to earth. "Do you know who Lillian married?" she asked anyway.

"I have no idea." James's brows creased in puzzlement. "Why do you ask?"

Maggie exchanged glances with Daisy, still hovering with the coffeepot. "No reason. I'm just curious since we were talking about her at the historical society meeting. She made hats."

"Now there's a lost art," James said. "Making hats. I've often wondered what I'd look like in a bowler hat. I had an uncle who always wore one." He made the gesture of settling a hat on his head.

Daisy eyed him with a narrowed gaze. "You'd look good in one," she decided. "Maybe we'll find some period clothes for men and you can be in our fashion show."

As she bustled off, James's mouth dropped open and he pointed at himself. "Me, in a fashion show?"

Maggie laughed. "Why not? It's for a good cause."

James shook his head. "You know how much trouble I've gotten into doing things for a good cause?" He picked up his egg sandwich and finished it off.

Enjoying the banter, Maggie settled back in her chair, warm mug of coffee in hand. At moments like this, she couldn't be happier.

A short while later, they were headed out of Somerset Harbor. "We're not going far," James said, "just a couple miles outside of town."

Maggie gazed out the window at the passing scenery. On one side of the road was the gray, wind-tossed bay, and on the other, rolling fields covered with patchy ice and snow. The trees were bare and brown, the only visual relief the green of pine, fir, and spruce. The land had a still quality, a sense of patient waiting for the renewal that would soon come.

"This is the toughest time of year," James said. "Having snow on the ground has gotten old, the holidays are over, and it seems like summer will never get here."

"You call it mud season here in Maine too, right?"

James skirted a pothole in the pavement. "We sure do. Some people say we have five seasons: spring, summer, fall, winter, and mud."

They shared a laugh, then Maggie said, "I heard one old salt say, 'We have nine months of winter and three months of poor sledding.'"

"That's about the size of it," James said, slowing the car. "Here's our turn." He pulled off the coast road onto a narrow lane. After about a quarter mile, Maggie saw a two-story white farmhouse and big red barn surrounded by fields. James turned into the driveway—the "dooryard," as Mainers called it—and pulled to a stop. Through open doors in the barn, Maggie glimpsed a late-model foreign station wagon with New York plates.

As was typical of many houses, the main building was attached to an ell, which in turn led to the barn. In the days when people kept cows and horses, they never had to step outside during the winter to tend them.

"This is a nice old place," James said as he turned off the engine. "But it needs a lot of updating. Fortunately, Jaime wants to keep its character, not just gut everything." James was committed to preserving historic structures in his work. He reached for his leather portfolio in the back.

"Jaime's the owner?" Maggie opened the car door, bracing herself for the blast of cold sure to greet her.

"Yes, Jaime Jones. She's a freelance magazine writer who moved here fairly recently."

They approached the kitchen entrance, reached via a small sunporch. James rapped on the door. The curtains twitched and then the door opened, revealing a slight woman in her thirties with pinned-up dark hair and pretty, elfin features. Her face lit up at the sight of James. "James. Come on in." She turned to

Maggie. "You must be Maggie. I've been meaning to come over to your shop. I need all kinds of furniture."

That comment warmed Maggie's heart. "Please do. You can also let us know if you need something specific and we'll look for it."

The kitchen they stepped into was definitely old-fashioned, and Maggie glanced around with interest. She loved old houses anyway, but knowing that Lillian had lived here made her more curious than usual. It looked like it hadn't changed at all since the 1940s. There was a huge porcelain sink on legs, a beast of a six-burner electric range, and only a few built-in cupboards.

"You can see why I'm remodeling," Jaime said with a laugh. "I love the big windows and the tall ceilings. And the hardwood floors, of course. But those appliances and sink have to go."

"You could definitely use more cabinets too," Maggie said. She spotted the Hoosier. "But that is really nice." It was a great specimen, made of oak, with cabinets that opened to reveal hoppers for flour and sugar and racks for spices. A tray pulled out to work on and handy cupboards and drawers were below. The set was complete with original containers for baking supplies.

Jaime ran a hand along the smooth wood. "It is cute. But I really don't need it. And when Chris told me about the great event you're planning for his grandfather, I knew exactly what to do with it." She grinned, a gesture that wrinkled her pert nose. "Give it to you."

Maggie didn't know what to focus on first, that Jaime knew Chris King or that she appeared to be donating the cabinet. "Wait, what?"

Jaime laughed. "Have a seat. I've got coffee if you want. Or tea."

Asking for coffee, Maggie and James sat at the table near the window. The view outside was of a side yard adorned with bird feeders on posts and hanging from a nearby tree. Birds of all sorts were hopping around on the ground and fluttering around the feeders.

Jaime brought over mugs of steaming coffee, a pitcher of milk, and a sugar bowl. She set a mug in front of another chair and joined them.

"So, as I was saying," Jaime said, "I want to donate the cabinet. I heard about the homeless shelter, and it's a very worthy cause." Her brow creased. "When I lived in New York, I saw homeless people everywhere. I even got to know some of them. It's really tragic."

"That is very generous of you," Maggie said. "The church can give you a donation letter at least." A cabinet like that was worth $1,000 or more.

Jaime shrugged. "Sure. That would be fine." She glanced around the kitchen. "I can't wait to get this place renovated. I love to cook, and it's really hard to function in here."

"I have the plans sketched out if you want to see," James said. He unzipped the leather portfolio and pulled out a sheaf of papers. Maggie and Jaime moved close to see what James had designed. The new kitchen included a deep farmhouse sink, recessed panel cabinets—some with glass fronts—and a new gas range and hood. Pendant lights gave a traditional but modern look.

"I love it," Jaime declared. "I can't wait to show Chris. He's really interested in what I'm doing here."

The mention of Chris again gave Maggie an opening. "So you know the Kings? I just met them while planning William's birthday celebration."

"We're both from Bangor but didn't meet until we were adults and both living here in Somerset Harbor." Stirring her coffee, Jaime gazed out at the birds as though remembering. "We ran into each other at the local bookstore, actually. I had ordered books for a novel I'm writing, and Chris was browsing the small-business start-up section. We got to chatting, and we've been dating ever since." She grinned. "I never saw myself taking up with a widower father, but his son, Trevor, is adorable."

Maggie was glad to hear Jaime liked Chris's son. Dating became much more complicated once you had children. She was thankful Emily was grown, not that Maggie planned on dating anytime soon. But if she did, at least she wouldn't be disrupting Emily's home life.

"He's thinking of forming a company?" James asked. "He should join the small-business group I go to. We have lunches once a month, and we exchange contacts and information plus encourage each other."

"Good idea," Jaime said. "Chris is kind of lost right now. He was a district manager in his father's business, and when they sold, he could have stayed on, but he didn't really like the corporate atmosphere. And he claims to be too old to go into the medical profession, like William, but I think he's just squeamish."

"James told me William's father was a carpenter," Maggie said. "Quite a few houses around here were built by the Kings. Maybe Chris would like to do something with his hands."

Jaime laughed. "He can try out home repair when I fix up the bedrooms. I can't afford to hire someone to do everything so I'm having James do just the kitchen and bathrooms."

"That's a wise move," James said. "Those rooms are what buyers look at."

"So I understand. But I never plan to sell this place." She sighed as she glanced around. "I feel such a connection to the past here. In fact, researching the previous owners is a pet project of mine."

Maggie's pulse leaped. "You'll be interested in this then. Ruth Harper's aunt used to live here. She made hats. And we think she knew a German spy." This last was her own conclusion, but she was sure the other women would concur that the note was related to the spies arriving in Maine.

Jaime's mouth was a perfect *O*. "Say that again. What's this about a spy?"

Maggie relayed how they'd found the note and her discovery that two German agents had landed on the Maine coast the same month and year.

The other woman clapped a hand to her head. "You aren't going to believe this." She pushed back her chair, leaped up, and rushed over to a set of drawers. She pulled the top one open and began to rummage. "I didn't think much of it. I hope I saved it . . ." With a cry of triumph she located an index card. "Here we go."

A recipe was written in faded blue ink on the worn, yellowed card. What startled Maggie was the name of the dish: *Kartoffelpuffer—Potato Pancakes.*

....

6

....

"Where did you find this?" Maggie asked. It wasn't that the recipe was for potato pancakes. Those were fairly common. It was the German name for them that caught her eye. She handed the card to James, who sounded out the foreign word with his lips moving silently, then shook his head.

"I found it in the Hoosier cabinet," Jaime said. "It was in one of the drawers with a lot of old papers." She leaned forward eagerly, clasping her hands between her knees. "Do you think it has something to do with the Germans?"

"It might," Maggie said. "I'm having the note translated. Maybe that will tell us what we need to know before we get too set on its meaning."

James had set the card on the table, and she picked it up and flipped it over. Unfortunately the back was blank—nothing written saying it was the favorite recipe of an espionage agent.

"I can't wait to know more." Jaime fairly bounced with anticipation.

"Are you thinking of doing an article?" While she understood the writer's excitement, Maggie wasn't sure how Ruth would feel about having her aunt's story published, especially if it turned out Lillian did help the spies for some reason. Maybe Maggie shouldn't have mentioned them. But then Jaime wouldn't have shared the recipe.

"I'm always thinking about new stories," Jaime said. "And you have to admit, this is very intriguing." She took a sip of coffee, cradling the cup in her hands. "I'm great at research, so let me know if you need help."

Maybe she could get information through Jaime without giving away too much. "That's a nice offer, thanks."

"There's still a lot of stuff up in the barn," Jaime said. "I'm planning to go through it this week. If I find anything interesting I'll let you know." She stood. "Anyone want another cup of coffee?"

James looked at Maggie. "I've got time if you do."

"We'll both take another cup," Maggie said. She smiled at James, grateful he was humoring her curiosity.

After collecting their mugs, Jaime popped a fresh pod into the single-cup coffeemaker and shut the lid, then pressed a button. "These are supposed to be so handy, but at times like this I wish I just had a pot of coffee. But most of the time it's just me here, and I don't want to try drinking whole pots by myself." She tapped her foot as she waited for the brewed coffee to trickle out.

"I can't imagine Daisy running The Busy Bean with pods," Maggie commented. Daisy had a coffee maker that held four pots as well as special equipment to make cappuccinos, espresso, and more.

"The Busy Bean? I love that place. Sometimes I take my laptop down there and sit and work. I love watching the boats go in and out of the harbor." Jaime pulled a full mug out from the maker and carried it to Maggie. She darted back to make one for James. "And Daisy is a hoot. I just love her accent."

"She's a good friend and a member of the historical society," Maggie said. "We're always looking for help with projects." Donations too, but Maggie didn't like to hit people with requests for money until they were engaged with the society.

"How about this? Once I sort through the barn, I'll let you select some things for the museum. And maybe I can meet with Ruth and learn more about her family and their life here on the farm."

"I'll ask her," Maggie said. "I'm sure she'll be flattered that you're interested."

"And I'll definitely consider an article about the new home-less shelter." Jaime's expression turned somber. "I'm so sorry to hear that Somerset Harbor has a homeless population too." She shivered. "I can't imagine not having a roof over my head during a Maine winter."

A while later, while driving back to town, James asked, "Are you up for a short detour?"

"You want to stop at another dealer?" Maggie glanced at the dashboard clock. It was past noon. "Or lunch maybe? I'm starving."

James laughed. "We did stay longer than I planned. Jaime's like that. I think it's the reporter in her. Before you know it, you're spilling your whole life story to her."

"Like mine, for instance?" During the last half hour of the visit, Maggie had found herself talking about her childhood summers visiting Aunt Evelyn in Somerset Harbor, her move to town after the loss of her husband, and Emily's attendance at St. Joseph's College. The reporter had listened intently, her eyes and small nods conveying interest and understanding.

"Your story reminded me: I think I saw you once, when you were with your aunt," James said in a musing tone. "I can't believe I never remembered it until today. You two were walking through town studying the various buildings."

"Where were you?" Maggie asked.

"Riding my bike. I was eight. You know, the age when you think girls are icky."

Maggie laughed. "I felt the same way about boys then. And yes, Aunt Evelyn and I used to take architecture walks, as she called them. She'd point out different features that would identify when a particular building was constructed and what period it was. I found it fascinating. Still do."

"So do I." James grinned. "Enough that I made a career out of it. How about The Lobster Quadrille for lunch? My treat."

"I'd love that."

"Can you hold out long enough for us to take a little side trip? It won't take more than fifteen minutes. And no, it's not stopping at an antiques dealer."

"All right. I'm game."

A couple of minutes later, James signaled and turned onto a side road leading toward the water. This road, which wasn't much more than a lane, was full of frost heaves and potholes, barely passable in some places. On both sides were scrubby woods in various dismal shades of gray and brown.

James had to slow to a crawl. "You can tell that hardly anyone comes down here. I'm not even sure they plow it."

Fortunately most of the snow had melted, so they were able to travel to where the road ended. As they got out, Maggie could hear surf breaking on the shore, but the view of the water was blocked by a hillside.

"This way." James led her across the small parking area to a path leading into the woods. Cans, bottles, and soggy paper were strewn on the ground and caught in the bushes, an indication this area wasn't popular except with those seeking privacy. Well-traveled beaches, parks, and shoreline were kept pristine by cleaning crews.

"Are you sure we should go up there?" Maggie asked. Unease made her spine prickle. There was something unpleasant about this place.

"We're not going far," James assured her. "Promise."

Shoving down her misgivings, Maggie followed, grasping an occasional tree trunk along the steep, slippery path to help her ascend. Ice and mud made the footing treacherous. They soon reached the top of the rise, and Maggie spotted a square white structure with a flat roof in the woods to her left. Another, much smaller square sat on top. "What's that?" she asked.

"It's a bunker. The Army used it during World War II to store ammunition and guns." He began to hike down the other side of the hill, cutting through the woods as he did so.

"Is that what you wanted to show me?" Maggie hurried to keep up, her feet sliding on pine needles.

"Yes. Isn't it great?" James picked his way around stumps and rocks and over fallen trees. "It's a real piece of history."

Maggie far preferred domestic history sites to those featuring war and violence. Many people loved battlefields, forts, and armories, but she wasn't among them. One thing her marriage had taught her, however, was to at least try to show interest in what fascinated someone you cared about. James was her friend, so she put a smile on her face and vowed to enjoy the experience.

James had reached the front door of the bunker, which had been built into the hillside. The upper vent must have been used to draw in air, Maggie decided.

"I used to bike over here all the time when I was a kid," James said. "My friends and I would pretend that we saw U-boats out in the bay and it was our job to defend the Maine coast."

Resting her hands on her hips, Maggie studied the concrete face of the bunker, then turned to face the water, imagining a submarine rising to the surface. The strife of World War II had always seemed so distant from America itself, an event that happened thousands of miles away in Europe and the South Pacific. Even the bombing of Pearl Harbor had taken place in Hawaii, five thousand miles from Maine.

But here on the East Coast, perhaps right on this rocky beach, enemy soldiers had landed. If America's line of defense hadn't been so strong, those first two spies might have paved the way for an enemy invasion.

"It makes you think, doesn't it?" James said as if he could

read her thoughts. "We weren't as safe here as we thought. The Germans were literally right out there." He pointed.

"I'm so grateful that we won that war," Maggie said softly. She thought about the intrepid Allied forces and how they had beaten back the Nazis, freeing captives and restoring countries to peace and rightful governments to power. Truly, good *had* overcome evil.

"I'm glad we're having a party for William," James said. "I think it's important to honor him."

"Me too. Let's make sure to invite Pop Welborn too." Samuel "Pop" Welborn was a retired Somerset Harbor High School history teacher. He was in his nineties and still sharp as a tack. Maggie reflected how two men who had served in the same war and were the same age could have such different mental states.

"Great idea," James said, jerking her thoughts back to the conversation. "And let's have someone read a list of deceased veterans from Somerset Harbor at the party."

Maggie felt a swell of emotion at this suggestion. So many of those brave men were gone. "Wonderful idea. We can ask Pastor David to read the list. Or how about you?"

"Pastor David," James said firmly. Although James was often in the public eye thanks to his role as alderman, it wasn't something he sought out.

Maggie took a step toward the bunker. "Have you ever gone inside?"

A sly smile flitted across James's face. "I cannot tell a lie. We did. But it was years back, when I was teenager."

They turned their attention back to the door, which was partially open. James pulled on it, making the opening wider. "Are you sure you want to go in?" he asked. "It's not that nice. Cold concrete with graffiti all over it."

"I'll just take a peek." They'd come this far. She might as well see what a bunker looked like inside. Maggie slid through the narrow opening. The first thing she noticed was the odor of woodsmoke. Then, when James pulled out a small flashlight and flicked it on, she saw something startling.

A bedroll, kerosene lantern, and cans of food revealed that someone had been staying inside the bunker.

Maggie stared at the pitiful arrangement, almost overwhelmed by shock and sympathy. The bunker was not only unheated, it was cold and dank and lacked windows. To use a fire, the door would need to be propped open to the cold. A prison cell would be a better environment than this.

"Is someone sleeping in here?" she asked James, knowing the answer full well.

"It appears so." James sounded grim. "Poor soul. We've got to get that shelter funded."

Maggie said, "I wonder who is staying here?"

"We aren't going to know unless we hang around until darkness falls," James said. "And there's no way to know whether someone would come back tonight at all. I'm sure whoever it is would prefer a bed at the shelter to the sleeping bag on this concrete. Or they might see that we've found their hideout and not come back for fear of getting in trouble for being in here without permission."

"I suppose." With a final look at the camp, Maggie turned toward the doorway. Although the day was frigid and overcast, the isolated beach felt more welcoming than this shelter.

On the way back to town, they were silent, lost in their own thoughts. Finally James spoke. "I'm as depressed as you are, Maggie. But all we can do is work hard to make the improved shelter a reality. So let's focus on that."

The Lobster Quadrille was on Shoreline Drive, next to the historical society building. The restaurant was quintessential

Maine with its rustic cedar siding and sailboat parked out front. Inside, the ceilings were draped with nets holding all manner of objects from the fishing trade and the sea. Maggie loved its quirky decor and welcoming atmosphere.

After hanging their coats, they approached the hostess station. "Two for lunch?" the young woman asked, grabbing two long menus out of the rack. Then she really looked at them and grinned. "Well, hello. How are you?"

Maggie recognized Jenny, who also worked at The Busy Bean. "I didn't know you were working here."

"I pick up a couple of shifts here now and then." Jenny led the way to a table by the front windows, which overlooked the wharf. "How's this?" They nodded, and she set the menus on the table. "Your waitress will be right over." With another grin, she bustled back to her post.

"Good kid," James said. "I've been talking to her about going to college, trying to give her pointers on applying for grants and scholarships." He picked up his menu and began to peruse it, although for Maggie and everyone she knew, there was typically a foregone conclusion for lunch—the lobster bisque.

"That's nice of you."

He shrugged. "She's smart. She should go to school."

"I hope she does." Maggie smiled to herself as she opened the menu. The better she got to know James, the more she found to admire about the man. His belief in giving to his community shone through his actions as well as his words.

The waitress hurried over, poured water into their glasses, and took their order—two servings of lobster bisque with a basket of hot homemade bread and hot coffee. The coffee and bread came first, with a promise the soup was right behind it.

As Maggie added cream to her coffee, she noticed a man sitting by himself. Ronald King. She thought of Emily's request that she speak to him about interviewing William. Well, there was no time like the present. Otherwise she might end up playing phone tag.

"Will you excuse me for a minute?" she asked James. "I need to speak to Ronald over there."

"Go right ahead. I'll hold down the fort." He reached for a hot roll and buttered it. "But don't be too long or these will be gone." He winked.

"I won't." Maggie put her napkin on the table and pushed back her chair. She approached Ronald from the rear so he didn't see her coming. When she skirted his table to stand in front of him, he glanced up in surprise. Maggie saw he was reading a thick tome that appeared to be an encyclopedia of medications. Was he ill or was this a professional pursuit? He'd owned drugstores—maybe he had an interest in pharmacology.

When he noticed her, he gave a laugh and tucked in a bookmark. "Just doing a little light reading. How may I help you?" By the blank look on his face, she guessed he didn't recognize her.

"I won't take much of your time, Mr. King. I'm Maggie Watson, a member of the historical society. I'm helping plan your father's party."

"Oh yes. I thought you looked familiar. It's going to be quite a shindig. Do you need my help with something?"

Maggie took a deep breath. "Not exactly. My daughter, Emily, and her friend Gina are students at St. Joseph's College. They're studying World War II and wanted to know if they could interview your father. If he's up for it."

"If the topic is the war, then he'll love it." Ronald's tone was dry. "You might have noticed that it's his favorite subject. Anything past 1945 is tough sledding to talk about with him."

"I'm sorry to hear that, Mr. King. It's hard watching a loved one decline."

"It is. Why don't you have your daughter call me and we'll set up a time." Ronald pulled a pen out of his inside jacket pocket and jotted a note on a business card. "This is my cell number." He nodded in dismissal. "Nice to see you, er . . ."

"Maggie. Maggie Watson." With a nod and smile, she turned and headed back to her table. Her bisque was just arriving.

"How'd it go?" James asked as she slid into her seat.

Maggie put the napkin back on her lap and picked up her spoon, inhaling the delicious odor wafting from the soup. "Great. My daughter and her friend are going to interview William King about World War II. It's a fabulous opportunity for her. I'm so glad Ronald agreed."

"Why wouldn't he?" James asked. "I'm sure his father will appreciate a chance to reminisce."

. . . .

On Friday afternoon, William answered the door when Maggie, Emily, and her friend Gina arrived at the King home, a Victorian house on one of Somerset Harbor's side streets. He was neatly dressed in a V-neck cardigan over a collared shirt with gray wool slacks, and he appeared clear-eyed and present. "Good afternoon, ladies," he said, holding the door open wide. "I've been looking forward to your visit."

"Thanks for having us," Emily said after Maggie introduced the girls to William. "And we're really looking forward to talking to you."

William made a comical face. "You want to talk to an old geezer like me? I guess miracles never cease." He chuckled, then held out his hand for their coats. "Let me hang those up." He settled each jacket in turn on the rack, adjusting them carefully. Once the garments were arranged to his satisfaction, he said, "We're visiting in the sitting room."

After showing them into a large room with a bay window and a fire cheerfully crackling in the fireplace, William rubbed his hands together. "I've got coffee or tea. Or would you prefer soft drinks? But young ladies don't like soda anymore, do they?" His brow creased in concern.

"Coffee is fine with us," Emily said. "What about you, Mom?"

Maggie moved closer to the fire and held out her hands to its heat. "Coffee sounds great."

After refusing their offers of help, William shuffled off to the kitchen, where the clanking of china was heard. The trio stood near the fire, warming up while waiting.

"He seems really nice," Emily said in a low voice. "I'm so excited about this."

"Me too," Gina said. She patted her handbag. "Do you think he'll let us film him?" She looked at Maggie.

"I have no idea," Maggie said. "You'll have to ask."

The clanking grew louder so they fell quiet, waiting for their host to join them. Humming under his breath, he carried in a tray and set it on a table. They spent the next few minutes doctoring their coffee with sugar and milk. After the silence extended a little too long, Maggie gave Emily a significant look and a nod.

Emily took a deep breath. "Dr. King, we were wondering. Do you mind if we film the interview? We want to share it with our class. If it turns out well, we'll put it online and in the library for other people to enjoy."

William quirked one brow. "You want to film me? I'm not exactly photogenic."

"That's all right," Gina said, then caught herself and blushed. "I mean, you're very handsome, but how you look doesn't matter. What counts is getting your story recorded."

William chuckled. "Don't worry about it, Gina. I was teasing.

Of course I don't mind being filmed." He set his cup down and sat up straight, his chest puffing out in pride. "I'm very flattered you asked me to share my stories."

After they finished the coffee, Emily had William sit in a wing chair in front of the fireplace. The camera was very small but it had a tripod, and Gina set it up fairly close to William.

"We'll sit off to the side and ask questions," Emily said. "Later, we'll edit the footage to take ourselves out. We want this to be more like informal storytelling than a Q and A session."

William clapped his hands on his knees. "I'm ready when you are." He peered at the digital camera. "I hope that thing's got plenty of film."

The girls laughed. "Don't worry, Dr. King. We have hours of memory," Gina said.

The elderly man smiled. "So do I."

. . . .

William King's Interview, Part 1

Before I tell you about my adventures overseas, I'd like to take a step back. You see, I was only sixteen when the Japanese bombed Pearl Harbor. I didn't enlist until I turned eighteen, in 1943. So I was kind of a latecomer to the war. But at home here in Somerset Harbor, we fought a different kind of battle.

My dad was called up right away. He was right at the upper age limit and had a family to support, but he had to go. That left me, my four younger siblings, and my mother. Dad built houses before the war. He made a good living, and he had winters off to indulge his passion for downhill skiing, which he shared with me. Unfortunately, I didn't inherit his skills as a carpenter, so I couldn't take over his business after he was called up. No one was building anyway. I might have scratched out some home repairs, but I was in high school and Mother wouldn't let me quit. She took a job down at the cannery to support the family. I did everything around the house—milked the cows, tended the garden, and chopped wood. I even took care of the animals when the vet couldn't get out to the farm.

Those were lean years, but for Maine farming families, it wasn't much different than before the war. They started rationing things, mainly certain kinds of food, gas, and clothes, but we'd always raised our own chickens and eggs and put vegetables away for the winter. No gas was tough for us, though. Mother had to drive the truck to work, so we kids rode our bicycles. In the winter, we cross-country skied or used snowshoes.

The hardest part was missing Dad and wondering if we'd ever see him again.

But others had it worse. Some families didn't have a strapping young son. They had to fend for themselves. And in the middle of a Maine winter, that was hard.

Our neighbor Lillian Spade was in that boat. Her parents died early in the war, and her brother and the hired man enlisted. Her sister was in the Army Nurse Corps. Poor Lillian had to sell all the cows except one. So I used to chop wood for her and help with some of the chores. In return, she did some sewing for my mother and sisters and of course she made them hats. The prettiest hats in church.

Lillian and I got to be quite good friends—who am I kidding? I was in love with her. She never knew, of course. She was an older woman, all of twenty-two.

So there we were, struggling along but keeping the young'uns fed and a roof over our heads. The war was always on our minds, coloring everything, kind of like the sun never shining. But it was miles and miles away, across the ocean.

Until the U-boats came. I remember the first time I heard about them being spotted, not too long after we entered the war. I didn't believe it at first but after a bunch of ships were torpedoed, I had to face it. Instead of relaxing by looking at the ocean, we were always straining our eyes for them, for one of those periscopes to stick up out of the water. The younger kids used to ask me if we were going to be invaded. Of course I said no, but I always felt like I was lying. I prayed I would be able to save them if something like that did happen.

Then the spies landed. And my escapade with Lillian began.

7

William's voice trailed off, and he closed his eyes, leaning his head back against the chair.

Emily jumped up, sending her mother a concerned look. "Mom, is something wrong with him?" She put one hand to her mouth, her eyes huge.

Maggie went to William's side and peered at the man, feeling somewhat intrusive, but also afraid he might be ill. She was glad to see his skin color was all right and his chest was rising and falling regularly. Then he gave a snort, and Maggie laughed in relief. "He's just napping. I guess we wore him out."

Footsteps came down the stairs and Chris appeared in the doorway. He quickly took in the situation. "Don't worry about Granddad. He's always nodding off." He smiled at the girls. "Were you doing your interview? Dad told me you were coming today."

"We were," Gina said. "And it was just getting good. He was telling us about some spies that landed in Maine."

Chris gazed fondly at his grandfather. "He's full of stories. They're amazing."

"Do you think we can do this again?" Emily asked. "There's so much more I want to know."

"Yeah, like what happened with the spies." Gina's eyes were alight with interest. "And Lillian."

"Lillian?" Chris cocked his head.

"She made hats. And your grandfather had a crush on her." Gina giggled.

Chris studied his grandfather as though trying to imagine him young and in love. He shook his head as if to clear it. "If

you want, we can set another date. I suggest you just do an hour
or two at a time."

"Will that work out with your schedule, Emily?" Maggie
asked. "They go to college at St. Joseph's," she explained to
Chris. "It's quite a distance."

"It's only an hour, Mom," Emily said. "Our professor wants
us to do research in the field. And we'll be over a lot to help with
Dr. King's birthday party anyway."

"How about tomorrow?" Gina suggested. "We're staying
over tonight." She grabbed Emily's arm. "In fact, let's stay for
the weekend. There's nothing much happening on campus
anyway."

Emily nodded. "That's a good idea. Is Dr. King available
tomorrow afternoon?"

Chris smiled. "Dr. King is available every day. Tomorrow
sounds great. Here?"

"How about coming over to Sedgwick Manor?" Maggie
suggested. "I'll feed you lunch."

After finalizing the arrangements to meet the next day, the
trio headed for home, Maggie at the wheel. "Guess what we're
having for dinner," Maggie said. "Lasagna." She'd pulled a pan
out of the freezer earlier in anticipation of Emily's visit.

Emily smacked her lips. "One of my favorites. Gina, wait
until you try my mom's lasagna. It's to die for."

"I can't wait," Gina said. "I'm starving."

Ah, the appetite of youth. "I've got snacks at the house too,"
Maggie said. "You two can forage when we get back."

"I have another idea," Emily said. "Why don't we look at
those 1940s clothes in the storeroom? We can pick out things for
the fashion show."

"Fashion show?" Gina's face was puzzled. "I thought we
were planning a birthday party."

Emily grinned. "A birthday party with an antiques auction, a fashion show, and a dance. It's going to be wild."

"I'll say," Gina said. "On my last birthday, my parents had a cookout." She crossed her arms with a mock pout. "I feel cheated."

"When you reach ninety, I promise I'll throw you a dance and a fashion show," Emily said. "Can you imagine what people will be wearing then?" She glanced down at her denim skirt and leggings. "They'll probably think these clothes are really weird."

The girls began chatting about what the clothes of the future might look like. Maggie considered taking a detour to stretch out the ride but knew Emily would notice since it was practically a straight shot back to the manor. She missed being the mostly invisible driver while her daughter and a friend shared confidences and insights.

Emily's phone dinged. She scanned the screen, then gave a hoot. "Mom, I got the translation back from the professor."

Maggie's heart gave a little leap. "Right there on your phone?"

"Yes, listen." Emily's head bent over the phone. "'*Dear Lillian, I will never forget how you saved my life. Please think of me with kindness, and God bless you always.*'"

"Who wrote that?" Gina's voice was a high-pitched squeak. "How intriguing."

"We don't know," Maggie said. "It wasn't signed. But we think maybe one of the German spies."

"A spy? Lillian saved a spy? Why would she?" Gina's pretty face was a study in confusion.

"We don't know. But I bet Dr. King does." Emily turned to face her mother. "Maybe we should change our project to this story. What do you think?"

Maggie was equally fascinated by the tale but knew she should advise caution. "I think it's worth exploring. Talk to your professor about it. Also wait and see if William does know more. He might not. If" —the words stuck in her throat—"if Lillian helped the Germans, she might have hidden it from him."

"I'm sure she would have," Emily said. "After all, it would have been considered treason."

Maggie's chest tightened as she thought of Ruth. "Another thing. I don't want to interfere with your project, but if we do find out Lillian committed treason, it would break Ruth's heart. Lillian was her aunt."

Emily sighed. "Oh, Mom, you're right. I'd hate to upset Ruth—she's such a sweetie. What are we going to do?"

Gina, in the back seat, piped up with the answer. "Let's see what Dr. King says first. Then we can decide. Worst case, we cover his service with the 10th Mountain Division in Italy. That's awesome too."

At the house, the girls eagerly greeted Snickers and then adjourned to the kitchen for the promised snacks. They nibbled on cheese, crackers, and veggies and dip while Maggie put together a salad and garlic bread for the evening meal.

"Look at this, Mom."

Maggie turned to see Emily holding a cat treat in the air. Snickers reared up on his back paws and took it gently in his mouth. Emily gave him another and Maggie laughed. "Are you training him or is he training you?"

"That's a good point," Gina said. "He's probably thinking, *All I have to do is stand up and this person will give me a treat.*"

Emily patted Snickers on the head. "We're training each other."

Maggie washed her hands and took off her apron. "Ready to go up to the storage room? We have time before dinner."

"I'd love to." Emily carried their dirty plates and cups to the dishwasher. "You won't believe the storage room, Gina. It's full of stuff from my family."

"That sounds like my closet," Gina said. "My sisters dump all the things they don't want to throw away in there."

"It's kind of the same thing," Maggie said. "I feel like an archaeologist whenever I go in there."

The storage room was a repurposed bedroom where Evelyn—and perhaps those before her—had archived furniture, clothing, household items, and other odd objects. The difference between this room and the attic, which was also full, was that these belongings had some kind of significance, either personal or historic.

In the upstairs hall, the girls paused to look down into the formal living room from the gallery. "I can't believe this house," Gina said. "It's amazing."

"I know," Emily said. "I'm still getting used to it." She threw her mother a smile. "It's a little bigger than our house in Vermont."

"Just a little," Maggie said. She'd loved the cozy little cottage she'd shared with her husband and daughter, but she also cherished the new memories made in Sedgwick Manor. She opened the door to the storage room. "Here we are."

"Whoa," Gina said. "This place is packed." Indeed, almost every square inch of floor was covered by something or other. Snickers wove his way through their legs and disappeared into the chaos.

"I hope we find Snickers again," Emily said with a laugh. She put her hands to her mouth. "Where are you, Snickers?" To their amusement, he appeared on top of a stack of hatboxes, which in turn rested on a wardrobe.

"The clothes are on that rack," Maggie said, pointing to the center of the room. A series of garment bags hung on a metal bar. "I haven't really examined all of them, but I do remember noticing some nice suits and dresses that looked to be from the '40s."

Emily scanned the room, taking in the placement of the obstacles between the door and the clothing. "I have an idea. Why don't we bring that out to the hall?"

"Are you sure?" Maggie regarded the room dubiously. "It's really wedged in there."

Emily pushed her sleeves up to her elbows. "Trust me. Moving furniture for three people into a dorm room meant for two taught me a few puzzle-solving skills."

While Maggie watched in bemusement, Emily and Gina rearranged the room, clearing a path for the bulky clothing rack. With one girl on each end, they pushed it out into the hall.

"Where are we going with this?" Gina asked.

"How about taking it to my room?" Emily's bedroom was quite large and had a standing mirror, which was perfect for trying on clothes.

They maneuvered the rack along the hallway and into the room with only a couple of mishaps, once when Gina pushed the wheel over Emily's toe and again when they bumped into an end table, sending an antique vase flying. Maggie caught it just in time.

After parking the rack, they began unzipping the bags, releasing the astringent odor of mothballs and old fabric into the air.

"Oh, Mom, look at this." Emily held up a cream silk organza dress embroidered with small flowers on vines. It had thin straps, a shirred bodice, and a long, sweeping skirt.

"That has got to be prewar, since it's silk," Maggie said. "It's gorgeous."

Gina had found an equally lovely gown in pink satin, with a halter neck and a square neckline. She held it up to herself, the color complementing her blonde hair and blue eyes. "What do you think?"

"I think it will be perfect on you," Maggie said. She reached out and rubbed the smooth fabric between her fingers, wondering why women had stopped wearing such lovely clothing. There wasn't a label. "I wonder if Barbara Sedgwick made these. She was quite a seamstress, apparently."

"Seriously?" Emily asked. "I thought they were made by a designer."

"My mom taught me how to sew and what makes a garment good quality," Gina said. She peered at the inside of the satin dress. "Look how tiny these stitches are. And see how even the gathering is around the waist?" She pointed out other features—perfectly flat facings, hand-stitched buttonholes, and a hem that hung perfectly.

They laid the gowns on the bed and kept looking. Emily selected a wool coat with a deep fur collar and a couple of trim wool skirt suits. Gina's finds included knickers and a jacket for winter sports and a dirndl skirt with a peasant-style blouse. In addition, there were a pair of overalls, a woman's sailor suit, and a pinafore dress with ruffles.

"Let's try these on," Emily said. She and Gina began to slide into the garments, one by one, admiring their reflections in the standing mirror. Maggie's role was to admire, help tweak a garment into place, and hang up discards again.

Gina struck a pose in the sailor suit, one hand on her hip. "The perfect outfit to wear when greeting your returning serviceman. He'll appreciate your patriotism and crisp good looks."

Emily twirled in the peasant skirt, sending it flying. "And when you're foraging in the fields for mushrooms to supplement your ration cards, consider wearing this little number. Your legs can move freely, and any cows you spot will feel like they're in Switzerland." She gave an energetic yodel.

They all burst into laughter. "For the most part, that was perfect," Maggie said. "Why don't you write your ideas down for the announcer at the fashion show?"

"We will." Emily slipped out of the skirt. "I want to try on a suit next." She pulled on a straight gray flannel skirt and buttoned a trim jacket. "Something like this would look perfect at a job interview."

"You can have it," Maggie said. "It fits you perfectly." Barbara Sedgwick must have been Emily's size.

"Thanks, Mom." Emily turned around to see the rear view, thrusting a hand into a pocket. Her brow creased. "What's this?" She pulled a narrow slip of paper out and unfolded it. Her eyes widened and she handed it to Maggie. "It's in German."

The paper read, *Deutsche Reichsbahn,* and appeared to be a wrapper for banknotes. Maggie folded it again. Yes, it would fit around a stack of paper money. "This is so strange. Why would Barbara Sedgwick have this in her pocket?" Somehow the piece of paper had survived cleaning and storage without being noticed.

Gina's eyes were like saucers. "Maybe it has something to do with those spies!"

8

....

G*ina could be right.* If so, that might mean Barbara Sedgwick had helped the Germans along with Lillian. Maggie swallowed a sudden lump in her throat, uneasy at the idea that Barbara might have been a traitor too.

Emily's voice jarred her out of her unhappy musing. "Mom, don't worry, we'll find out the truth. I'm sure Lillian and Barbara were innocent."

Maggie rose to her feet. "I hope you're right. Let's get these things put away and then we'll have dinner." Not that she had an appetite anymore.

While the girls hung the clothing for the show in the bedroom closet and moved the rack back into the storage room, Maggie went downstairs to check on the lasagna and put the garlic bread in the oven. The house phone in the kitchen rang, an old-fashioned wall model that dated to Evelyn's time and always brought Maggie back to her childhood.

It was Ruth. "Maggie, so glad I caught you. I've been thinking about the buffet dinner and serving dishes made under rationing. I remember Evelyn telling me that she had some old family cookbooks from that period."

Tethered by the curly cord, Maggie could only move so far. "I can check when I get off. The cookbooks are in a cupboard across the room." With her love of all things old, Evelyn had collected cookbooks from the early 1800s to the present day.

"That would be great. I'll be searching mine too. Once we decide on a menu, we can divvy up the cooking chores. And The Busy Bean and The Lobster Quadrille will help." The two restaurants often supported charity events by donating food.

"I'll look through them tonight," Maggie promised. The girls would undoubtedly get a kick out of helping choose dishes for the dinner. They seemed to be enjoying their research into World War II history.

"How did it go with William King?" Ruth asked. Maggie had mentioned Emily's project to Ruth and the other members of the historical society.

Maggie was lost for words for a moment. It was on the tip of her tongue to tell Ruth about William bringing up the spies. In addition, she should tell her what the translated note said, as well as about Jaime's German recipe and the banknote wrapper in Barbara's pocket. But if she shared all that, she would only worry Ruth. Surely it was better to wait until they knew the whole story.

"It went great," Maggie said finally, just before the silence grew awkward. "It was kind of a short session since William was tired, but we're going to schedule more." It would have been rude to mention William falling asleep. *No sense in sharing that embarrassing episode with anyone.* She'd have to caution the girls not to talk about it.

"I can't wait to read it," Ruth said. "They're writing a story, right?"

"Actually, they're filming it," Maggie said.

"Even better. We'll get a copy and include it in our display at the museum. We can also show it during the birthday party."

Maggie's heart sank at these suggestions, which of course were perfectly reasonable. Under other circumstances, the video would be a nice addition to the museum and the party. She imagined William saying "Then the spies landed" to a packed room and her stomach turned over. Maybe she could claim the video was missing or damaged . . . She took a deep breath and rallied. *Calm down. The girls will just have to edit the film to only his battle stories.*

"We'll have to see if it's ready by then, but yes, it would be a great touch." Struck by inspiration, Maggie thought of a way to shift focus off of William. "Speaking of the exhibit, I have some items we can add. The girls were just trying on Barbara Sedgwick's clothing for the fashion show, and there are some wonderful outfits. Why don't we put some of the pieces on display at the museum after the party?"

"Oh, what a lovely idea, Maggie," Ruth said. "That will really fill things out."

Relieved to be off the topic of spies, Maggie chatted a little more with Ruth, hanging up as the girls trooped into the kitchen.

"Do you want us to set the table?" Emily asked on her way to the cupboards.

"Please. Let's eat in here. It's cozy." Maggie forced a smile to her face. "Plus we have a new project. We're going to find some yummy World War II recipes using rationed items."

Gina cocked a brow. "Do *yummy* and *rationed* belong in the same sentence?" She followed Emily, who pointed her to the silverware drawer.

"We'll find out," Maggie said. "We'll need to test them before inflicting them on the general public." She pictured a line of gelatin molds and canned meat dishes lining the buffet table and shuddered.

"That sounds fun," Emily said. "You know how much I love to eat." She placed colorful pottery plates on the table, Gina coming along behind with forks and knives.

"I know." Maggie slid her hands into oven mitts and pulled the piping-hot, bubbling lasagna out of the oven and set it on the stove. "Let's have salad while this rests for a few minutes." She reached in again for the garlic bread.

"How long?" Emily grabbed her belly. "The smell is making me crazy."

"Ten minutes." Maggie opened the fridge and grabbed the salad and a selection of dressings. "Go ahead and dig in."

After they finished and cleaned up, Maggie perused the line of cookbooks and chose several printed in the 1940s.

"What we're looking for are recipes that we can make for a crowd," Maggie said. "We'll test some of them out ourselves first to make sure they taste good."

Emily chose a book and began leafing through. "I definitely think we should. Eggless cake?" Her nose wrinkled. "How good can that be?"

"How about this one?" Gina asked, pointing. "Cake without butter, eggs, or milk."

"What's left?" Maggie asked with a laugh. "Flour?" She'd never made a cake without eggs or butter. Milk was sometimes optional.

Gina scanned the page, reading out loud, "Basically, water, brown sugar, raisins, flour, and spices. And lard. What is that?"

"Fat from a pig," Maggie said. "The old-timers often used it instead of butter before vegetable shortening was created."

"Ew, really?" Gina shook her head. "My mom would never go for that."

"Here's some advice about a buffet supper." Emily began to read. "'Even on special occasions, a simple dinner is in keeping with the times.'" She laughed. "I love the quaint wording." She kept going. "'Start with fruit or vegetable juices, fresh fruit cups, or cheese puffs. Select economical cuts of meat and serve them with savory sauces. Homemade condiments, pickles, and jellies along with fresh bread will add delicious touches.'"

"Now we're on the right track," Maggie said. "Do they suggest specific dishes?"

Emily's lip curled. "Yes. Sliced tongue." Gina gave a shriek, and both girls began giggling and making exclamations of disgust. "And what about—drumroll, please—stuffed beef heart?" Their merriment was even louder.

"Organ meats were cheap alternatives," Maggie said, suppressing a shudder. "Like kidneys and sweetbreads."

"Ugh, no, Mom." Emily grabbed her belly with both hands.

"I'm guessing 'sweetbreads' doesn't refer to actual bread," Gina said. "Yuck."

"All right, moving on." Maggie studied the recipes. "Meat loaf sounds too ordinary. And creamed oysters? I guess what wasn't a luxury then is out of our reach now. We can't afford oysters for hundreds."

Gina said, "How about chicken à la king?" Her face lit up. "That would be perfect for Dr. King!"

"It would be," Maggie said. "And Welsh rarebit is a good dish. It's basically melted cheese on toast."

"Everyone loves cheese," Emily said. "Let's do some of these molded salads. They look cool." She held up the page so they could see the photographs of brightly colored gelatin salads filled with various vegetables and garnished lavishly.

"This is really good for a start," Maggie said. She marked the recipes with slips of paper. "If you want, you can look through the cupboards and see if we have molds for the salads." She pushed back from the table. "I think I'm going to read Aunt Evelyn's journal again. I want to see what else she says about Barbara Sedgwick."

"All right, Mom. After we do that, we'll probably need to get to some homework."

"If you want dessert, there's ice cream." Maggie poured a glass of ice water and took it with her to the office, Snickers at her heels. He jumped into a leather wing chair and curled up, tail touching his nose. Maggie settled behind the desk and pulled out the journal.

Ever since finding the banknote wrapper, she had felt unsettled and on edge. Whatever had happened during March of 1943 in Somerset Harbor, it appeared to be a little-known story until now, when William agreed to be interviewed. If not, Ruth, Ina, or Deborah surely would have heard about it from their mothers or directly from Lillian herself. Unless they were trying to keep it hidden. Maggie wouldn't blame them for that.

Evelyn's journal entries weren't always in an order Maggie would find logical, although she was sure the system had made sense to her departed aunt. She had to carefully study the family section of the book to find the information she sought — wartime love letters between Barbara and Andrew Sedgwick were somewhere in the storage room.

Maggie glanced at the mantel clock. *After nine. Should I tackle that now?* She thought about the crowded mass of boxes and sighed. It could take hours, and in addition, the lighting in that room wasn't the best. Snickers stretched, giving a huge, yowling yawn. Maggie laughed. "My sentiments exactly. Let's go read a book in bed."

· · · · · · · · · · · · · · · · ·

The next morning, Maggie awoke refreshed, her mood enhanced by the sunshine streaming into the room once she opened the curtains. Icicles on the roof were melting in the warmth, water dripping down like arrows of light. It was early, just before eight, so she decided to let the girls sleep in. After a quick breakfast of scrambled eggs, she got dressed and headed up to the storage room, Snickers accompanying her.

Maggie sighed when she surveyed the room, intimidated as always by the task of sorting through its contents. Then she had an idea. Why not write down what she found in each box and tape it to the top? That way, future expeditions would be more efficient and less time-consuming.

After fetching index cards, a pen, and tape from the office, she set to work, jotting down what she found as she went. After opening and shutting a dozen boxes, a standing wooden sewing basket caught her eye. Maybe it had belonged to Barbara.

Maggie tugged on the knobs on top and the basket opened, folding out to reveal compartments. Inside was a treasure trove of vintage sewing supplies she couldn't resist exploring. She found spools of thread, cards with hooks and eyes and snaps, packs of needles, and a strawberry pincushion. An old candy tin held buttons. She pried it open, relishing the mix of antique buttons—their bright colors, interesting designs, and range of materials. Modern versions were pretty boring in comparison.

An odd shape caught her eye, a diamond-shaped piece of metal with two "arms" to fasten it on clothing. She'd known someone in the military who'd had them on his uniform, something called a pip, which denoted rank. She put the piece back in the button box and pushed on the lid. She'd take these downstairs and put them with her sewing kit, which admittedly was pretty meager. She could always use more buttons.

In the bottom of one of the trays was a photograph of a handsome, dark-haired man in uniform. She turned it over. *Captain Andrew Sedgwick, my darling husband.* She smiled. *How sweet.* Barbara had kept his photograph nearby as she stitched. Maggie dug through the bottom tray, moving aside packets of binding and lace. Her fingers touched a bundle of papers. *Could it be? Yes.* She had found the letters, tied together with faded red ribbon.

9

Leaving the bundle tied, Maggie leafed through the envelopes. By the return addresses, it looked like letters both to and from Andrew. By some miracle, Andrew must have managed to keep her letters with him through the war. *What a wonderful record of a couple's relationship during a very difficult time in history.*

Maggie thought about taking only the letters down but hesitated. *Why not use the basket?* It would look perfect beside her chair in the library. Every time she sewed on a button or mended a hem, she would feel connected to Barbara, another mistress of Sedgwick Manor.

Maggie clicked her tongue to beckon Snickers, who was lurking underneath an old rocking horse, and rose to her feet with a groan. Time to have another cup of coffee—and to read the letters.

"Mom?" Emily called as Maggie went by her bedroom door.

Maggie set down the basket and opened the door a crack. Snickers darted in and ran toward Emily. "Good morning. Sleep well?"

Emily stretched with a yawn. "Sure did." She motioned her head toward the open door to the adjoining room, where Gina was curled in a ball in bed. Only the top of her head was visible above the covers. "So did she apparently."

"What would you like for breakfast?"

Emily's grin was gleeful. "Waffles." She had loved waffles since childhood, not that her figure ever reflected it. "With maple syrup." She turned on her side to pet Snickers, who had jumped onto the bed.

He and I both love having her around. "Coming right up."
Maggie shut the door, picked up the basket, and continued on
her way.

In the kitchen, she pulled out the waffle iron, an antique
striped mixing bowl, and the ingredients. She didn't even have
to consult a recipe since she'd made these more mornings than
she could count.

Emily, with her impeccable sense of timing, trailed into the
kitchen as Maggie was lifting the first batch out of the iron. She
sniffed. "Smells awesome." She took the plate and sat down in
the breakfast nook, where butter and syrup waited.

"Is Gina coming?" Maggie closed the lid so the iron could
warm up again.

"She'll be right down. Snickers is still up there, sleeping on
my bed."

Maggie added batter to the grill. "I found letters between
Barbara and Andrew Sedgwick this morning."

Emily paused in the act of cutting her waffle with her fork.
"Really? Did you find anything about the spies in them?"

"I haven't had a chance to look. I thought we could do that
after breakfast." Maggie heard footsteps on the stairs. "Here
comes Gina. We also have to decide on a lunch menu. William
and Chris are coming over."

"That's right. I'm excited to film another installment of Dr.
King's story." Emily took a big bite of golden waffle. After she
swallowed, she said, "How about clam chowder and bread? I
can run down to the docks for fresh clams and stop by the Bean
for bread."

Maggie glanced at the clock. "You'll have to go soon. They're
coming at one." Emily's suggestion was a good one, since chowder
didn't have to simmer for hours to taste good. The next waffle
was done. "Another?"

Emily nodded. "Please. I'll go downtown right after I eat and shower. I hope we can look through the letters before the Kings come. I'm dying to see if there's anything in them."

"Me too." Maggie turned to Gina, who came into the kitchen looking barely conscious but cheerful. "Good morning. Sleep well?"

"I sure did," Gina said. "It's so quiet here." She headed for the coffeepot, not standing on ceremony. It warmed Maggie's heart that the girl felt at home here.

"Waffle coming right up," Maggie said. "Maybe you can help me set the dining room table for lunch while Emily does an errand, Gina. Then we'll have time to at least glance through the letters before they come."

Gina turned around, mug in hand. "Letters?"

"Mom found some World War II letters between Barbara Sedgwick and her husband," Emily explained.

"That's exciting. I feel like we're investigating a real mystery." Gina sat at the table, smiling up at Maggie as she set a plate in front of her. "Thanks, Mrs. Watson. This looks wonderful."

"Yes, thanks for everything, Mom." Emily said. She turned to her friend. "Isn't she the best cook?"

Maggie smiled as she put another waffle on for Gina. She might not see her daughter as often as she'd like, but she'd savor every moment they had together.

"I'll say," Gina said, lavishing maple syrup on her waffle. "So much better than the dining commons at school."

After the girls were finished, Emily got dressed and went shopping while Gina helped get the dining room ready. At her suggestion, they put together a centerpiece of holly leaves and evergreen boughs, the only green plants at this time of year.

After Emily got back from her errands, she set up the camera in the library, the spot they'd chosen for today's interview with William King, and then all three returned to the kitchen.

"These deserve a much more leisurely and careful reading than we have time for just now," Maggie said regretfully, untying the bundle of letters. "But let's see if there is anything from March or April 1943."

They ended up separating the letters into two piles, by sender. Then, while Maggie started the chowder, the girls put them in chronological order.

"Barbara wrote two in March and one in April," Emily said. She handed one letter each to Maggie and Gina.

Maggie slid the letter out of the envelope with both curiosity and the sense she was prying into the life of a couple long dead. Almost nothing was more intimate than their correspondence, read only by them. Then she noticed a stamp on the envelope. *And the censor of course.* Wartime mail was frequently opened and read, and if the censor found a passage deemed too sensitive, the passage was literally cut out with scissors. *What a massive, fascinating, and possibly embarrassing task that had been.*

This letter was dated March 30. Maggie scanned the text, her pulse racing as she came upon the words, *Your activities are classified, darling. I accept that. But what would you say if you learned that recently your dull little wife has been involved in quite an exciting affair?*

"I've got something," Maggie said. "Listen." She read aloud the sentences she'd already seen and then continued, "'I can't tell you the particulars, but I will share them when you come home. Suffice it to say that for a week or two, tiny Somerset Harbor was the site of wartime action, beginning when—" Maggie groaned. The censor had cut out the rest of the sentence.

"That's it?" Emily asked. "I was hoping that letter would tell us what happened with the spies."

"What a bummer," Gina said with a pout. "But at least we still have Dr. King to interview."

Maggie, on her way back to the stove to check the chowder, halted at a realization. "You know, William could be the only person left who witnessed the spies firsthand. I think Pop Welborn was overseas at that point, and it's entirely possible that everyone else is gone."

Emily nodded slowly, her face solemn as this idea sank in. "That really makes you think, doesn't it? I'm so glad we're doing interviews with him. We need to capture his memories."

William and Chris King arrived promptly at one and the group sat down to lunch. Maggie served out big bowls of chowder, and Emily passed around heated rolls and butter. Gina served ice water and coffee.

"It's not a bad day," Chris said. "Finally a break in the weather."

William chuckled. "Don't be fooled. There's a storm coming. That's how March is. Winter always has the final word." He tasted the soup and smiled with appreciation. "This is very tasty, young lady," he said to Maggie.

Everyone probably seems young when you're ninety, Maggie reflected. "I'm glad you like it. Clams were fresh today."

"That's one thing I love about living on the coast," Chris said. "Fresh seafood. I could eat it every day."

"There were times we had to," William said. His voice rose in imitation of a child's high-pitched tones. "'No, Mom, not lobster again!'"

The girls laughed. "Was that during the war?" Gina asked.

"The Great Depression," William said. "During the war, we had chicken—lots of chicken."

"Beef was rationed, right?" Emily said. "Back then, you were forced to eat healthy. Red meat was restricted."

"That's one way of looking at it," Chris said. "You could sell a book, *The Ration Diet*. You'd make millions."

"Take notes, Gina," Emily said. "That's a great idea."

The lunch went on like that, with plenty of friendly banter and jokes. Afterward, Chris and Maggie had another cup of coffee while Emily and Gina settled William in the library.

"By the way, James Bennett and I met with Jaime Jones the other day," Maggie said. "She said she knows you."

His face lit up. "Yes, we met a few months ago here in town. She told me she was donating the Hoosier cabinet for the auction."

"She did, and it's lovely." Maggie took a sip of coffee. She thought of something else to chat about. "Did your son enjoy the card tricks Ace did during the dinner?"

Chris laughed. "He loved them. The other night, he spent three hours online reading up on how to do card tricks. When I dropped him off at his friend's house earlier, he told me he was going to practice so he could be as good as Ace."

Maggie thought back to Ace's skilled handling of the cards, almost breathtaking at times. "He was impressive with those cards, that's for sure."

Chris twirled his spoon around on the tablecloth. "Seeing those homeless men and women really touched my heart. It's so sad that they're not with their families. If they have families, that is. I suppose some of them don't."

"It really bothers me too," Maggie said. "We're working on a bigger shelter, but somehow I think that's just a drop in the bucket."

They were silent a moment, Chris staring out the window at the sunny day. Then he shook himself. "Sorry. I didn't mean to drift off like that. It's just . . ." He fell silent again, then gave a big sigh. "My father disappeared years ago from Bangor. My biological father, that is. Ronald adopted and raised me, and he's been wonderful. There he was, a single guy with a business, taking on me, a messed-up kid."

"I'm sorry to hear about your biological father," Maggie said. "That must be hard."

"It is. There was a terrible accident one night. I don't remember it at all. Probably because I was asleep in the back seat and then I hit my head in the crash. My mom died, and my dad was badly hurt, physically and from the pain of losing my mom." His features tightened in distress. "I can't really remember his face or his voice clearly. Or Mom's. It's like the harder I try to recall them, the more they slip through my grasp."

"I'm so sorry to hear about your loss." Maggie's heart ached with sympathy for this man who had basically lost both parents and, from what she had gathered from Jaime, his wife as well. "And it's natural to want to see your father. No one knows where he is?"

Chris shook his head. "When he finally got out of the hospital several years ago, he didn't come home. Ronald told me he didn't tell the facility where he was going, but he had left behind a few books about Florida. He gets angry whenever I mention Dad, so I dropped it." He was silent for a minute and Maggie didn't speak, sensing he had more to say. "Seeing the homeless men kind of brought up the whole thing again. I wonder, is he homeless? Is he hurting?" He ducked his head, face creasing with pain. "Is he dead?" The last was a whisper.

Maggie reached out and touched his sleeve. "Why don't we look for him?"

Hope lightened his features briefly before he sank into gloom again. "The last time we talked about it, years ago, Ronald said he had a detective on the case. He came up short."

"It won't hurt to try again," Maggie said. "My friends and I are pretty good at ferreting out information."

"Would you really do that?" The hope was back, shining in his eyes. "I'd love nothing more than to introduce Trevor to his grandfather. My dad might have had his problems, but he was a wonderful father before the accident. I remember that much."

"Let's exchange contact info," Maggie said. "I'll do some research and let you know what I find out."

Chris took out his cell phone and entered Maggie's home and cell phone numbers. She did the same.

Emily put her head around the doorjamb. "We're ready if you want to listen in."

. . . .

William King's Interview, Part 2

There was a snowstorm the night the spies landed, a few miles north of here. Later, officials pieced together the story. The U-boat had lurked off the coast for days. At the right time, in the dead of night and bad weather, the two German agents rowed to shore in an inflatable raft.

From there, they were to make their way to New York City. The men picked their way across the sandy beach and then, carrying suitcases, headed along to the road toward the village. The idea was they would catch an early train. The cover story? They were two visitors from out of town whose car had broken down.

One person did see them trudging along. Doris Linton was on her way back from visiting a sick relative the next town over. You should have seen Doris once she realized she could have captured the spies just by offering them a ride. But although she was a brave and adventurous woman, she knew better than to let strange men into her automobile.

Doris didn't call the police and so, if things hadn't gone wrong for the Germans, they might have made it to New York without incident.

The first thing that interfered was the snowstorm, which turned into a blizzard. A real record-breaker—over forty inches of snow and winds up to seventy miles per hour. Apparently the German weather forecasting service wasn't terribly accurate.

A day and night went by and still the storm raged on. Even in town people were trapped in their houses. Out in the country, where Lillian and I lived, we were even more isolated. At times like that you thank God for a cellar full of preserves, lots of firewood, and a barn that's connected to the house.

As I said, Lillian lived alone and so it was up to her to milk the cow twice a day. Cows don't like it if you neglect them. Plus Lillian was able to make her own butter, which was rationed otherwise.

Early the second dawn after they landed, Lillian was milking away, sitting on a stool and shivering in the cold. Although the barn was warm enough for the cow and chickens, it was far colder than she liked. Outside, the storm howled on, wind pushing snow through the cracks in the walls. The gusts were so strong that at times the lantern hanging overhead swayed.

Lillian heard a strange sound, a shuffling noise, then a whimper. She spun around on the stool, expecting to see a wild creature taking shelter, maybe a raccoon or fox. She hoped it wasn't sick, having emerged from its burrow the previous week when the temperatures had warmed.

Instead, her heart practically stopped when she saw a man slump against the wall, his hand clasped to his right arm, which was red with blood.

"Hilf mir, bitte."

He was speaking German.

10

As during the first interview, William appeared to tire, but he didn't go so far as to fall asleep. He reached his hand out to Chris. "I think it's time for these old bones to go home."

"Right away, Granddad," Chris said. He turned to Emily and Gina. "We'll do another session soon." He grinned. "I'm as interested as you to find out what happened. He's never told me this story before."

"That's because the time wasn't right," William said. He levered himself out of the chair and Chris darted forward to help, allowing the older man to grasp his forearm. The duo said goodbye to Emily and Gina, then went to the hall, where they donned their outerwear.

"I'm so glad you could come over," Maggie said, opening the front door for them. A blast of cold air hit her and she peered up at the sky, which had clouded over. "It's snowing!"

"What'd I tell you, boy?" William chuckled. "I may be a dinosaur but I can call 'em."

"I'll listen to you next time, Granddad." Chris helped William down the stairs and to their car. With a wave, they got in.

Maggie shut the front door and went to join the girls. They were reviewing the footage on Emily's laptop.

"Mom," Emily said, her voice rising in excitement, "do you believe that story? Lillian did encounter the spies. Or one of them at least."

"And who do you suppose hurt him?" Gina asked. "I can't wait to find out."

"This is more exciting than any television show," Emily said, turning her attention back to the screen. "And it's real."

"Real life is full of great stories," Maggie said. "Changing the subject, any ideas about what I should make for dinner?" Although she loved to cook, especially for others, sometimes she lacked inspiration.

"How about shepherd's pie?" Emily suggested. "It's one of my favorites."

Maggie thought about the ingredients needed: ground beef, mushrooms, onions, potatoes, peas, and corn. She had all of them. "I can do that."

"Great. We'll make a salad to go with it."

Maggie put on the kettle. Outside the kitchen window, the snowflakes swirled. It was only three o'clock, so if she put together the casserole now, she could start researching for Chris online. She had a feeling, though, that she might need to make a trip to the library or the newspaper archive. Many articles written before the widespread use of the Internet were not digitized yet. They were still in microfilm or even paper form.

Her cell phone chimed, indicating she had a message. *Found some of Lillian's things that you'll want to see. Come out this afternoon if you want. Jaime.* She didn't recognize the number, but this was her first text from the reporter.

Research online could wait. Learning what Jaime had found sounded more exciting. And she could use a reason to get out of the house, even if it was snowing.

Be there at four or so, she wrote back.

Forty-five minutes later, Maggie left the house, the rest of dinner in Emily's capable hands. A light dusting of flakes covered her car, so Maggie brushed it off before getting in. The snow was steady, insistently flowing down to cover the roads, almost-bare grass, and rooftops. Dusk was coming early with the lowering clouds and gloom as the bad weather settled in. According to the forecast, she had just enough time to visit Jaime and come home before the worst hit.

Saturday afternoon traffic was light, with most people already home for the evening due to the weather. Smoke streamed out of chimneys, and brightly lit windows gave glimpses of families gathered around kitchen tables or seated in comfortable living rooms.

Maggie glanced at the fuel indicator. *When did I last get gas?* She had a comfortable half a tank. Then her eye fell on the temperature gauge. *Is it higher than normal?* She wasn't quite sure, but it was well below the red zone, so she figured she should be all right. She'd keep an eye on it and have the garage check the coolant level when she had a chance.

The lights of Somerset Harbor faded as Maggie took the coast road. Here homes were few and far between. Jaime was only a couple of miles out, so it didn't take long to reach her house. Lights winked cheerfully in the farmhouse as Maggie pulled up the driveway. After hearing William's story, she looked at the property in a new light. *Lillian encountered a spy right there in that barn.*

Then Maggie noticed the barn door was open, and the station wagon was gone. *That's odd.* But maybe Jaime's car was being repaired. Maggie shut off the Jetta's engine and climbed out, already looking forward to getting home again. Glancing up at the sky, she noticed that the snow was thickening. Wind howled around the corner of the barn, striking Maggie with such force that she staggered.

She hurried for the kitchen door, eager to get inside. She rapped once, then again. Nothing. Jaime wasn't home. Annoyed, she got back inside the car and sent a text. *I'm here. Are we still meeting?*

No answer. Maggie thrust down her irritation. Maybe Jaime had an emergency and hadn't thought to contact her, or maybe she hadn't had time. She reached to start the car and then paused. Why not leave a note? Foraging through her handbag, she found an old receipt and a pen, then wrote, *Sorry I missed you. Please give me a call. Maggie.* She wedged it in the storm door, hoping Jaime would see it.

Hopping back into the car, she eased down the driveway and onto the main road, deserted now as a curtain of driving snow came down, reducing visibility to almost nil. The Jetta rocked, buffeted by gusts, and Maggie was forced to slow to a crawl so she wouldn't lose control on the slippery pavement.

Despite her low speed and the fact that she wasn't pushing the engine, the temperature gauge continued to climb. Maggie flicked glances at it, knowing that if she took her eyes off the road too long, she might slide into the ditch. She crept up a hill toward the crest. Here she slowed even more, anticipating that she would pick up speed as she descended. Using the brakes on icy roads was not advisable, as it could send the vehicle into a slide.

She had almost made it down the hill when her wheels hit a patch of ice and the car fishtailed. Heat flashed over her face and her stomach dropped as she worked to bring the car under control. She heard Richard's voice reminding her to steer in the direction of the skid.

Maggie finally got the car under control and moving in a straight line again. Relief washed over her, making her weak. Then she saw the temperature gauge. The indicator had soared into the red zone. If she kept driving, she would ruin her engine.

A slight pull-off was just ahead. Maggie eased the car into the spot and shut off the engine. The cooling engine ticked. Wind howled. Snow hissed down, bits of ice pinging against the windows.

Maggie dug her phone out of her handbag. No bars. She tossed the phone onto the passenger seat. *Now what?* She was far from town on a deserted road with a car she didn't dare to drive and no cell service. In a blizzard, no less.

Slumping back against the headrest, she laughed. *What else can I do? This is absurd. The perfect storm of bad luck.*

The air was rapidly cooling so Maggie reached behind her seat and pulled out the space blanket her husband had insisted she always carry. There was a book of matches and a candle wrapped in it, which would actually heat the interior of the car if lit. She unfolded the crinkly silver blanket and tucked it around her body, leaving her hands free to light the candle. She'd wait on that a little. She hoped someone would come along soon.

Staring out into the storm, Maggie prayed. *Please send help. Don't let the girls worry too much.* She pictured them at Sedgwick Manor, looking at the clock and wondering where she was. If they tried to call, they wouldn't get through, not while she was stuck in this hollow. *Maybe they'll send a search party.* But not for hours. They would assume that she was tucked safely inside Jaime's kitchen and had to stay there because of the storm. They didn't have the reporter's number.

In frustration, Maggie thumped the steering wheel with her fist. How many times had she told Emily to leave a number to her destination? From now on, she would definitely do the same. Not that it would help right now, with Jaime out, but in most circumstances it would. As she so often lectured Emily, cell phones die or sometimes don't work. People get into accidents—or break down.

In the middle of nowhere. It was over a mile to a house in any direction, and it wasn't safe to walk in a blizzard, with its low visibility, wind chill factor, and drifting snow. That had been drilled into her head as a child, with tales of people dying within mere feet of their homes.

She jerked her mind back from wandering thoughts, worried that hypothermia was setting in. *What if I'm here all night? They'll find me in the morning, frozen in a seated position.* If enough snow fell fast enough, the snowplows couldn't keep up. Remote houses were sometimes snowed in for days.

Maggie's chest tightened, making her breathing come in gasps. She noticed her fists were clenched, her shoulders tight.

Light the candle.

After fumbling with the matches, she took off her gloves and lit the candle, placing it inside a tin can reserved for that purpose. Then, fingertips numb, she gratefully pulled the gloves on again. The brave little light flickered like a beacon of hope, comforting her. She found a bottle of water and drank some.

Maggie had gone all the way through her prayer list and was starting a second round when the impossible happened. Two glowing lights appeared, piercing the veil of snow. Someone was coming!

Rather than get out, she turned the key and put on the flashers. Then she honked the horn in a staccato beat, in time with the flashers.

Stop, please stop! Don't drive by!

Mercifully, the vehicle halted. Tears sprang to her eyes. She opened the door and got out, waving her arms. The driver's-side window rolled down.

"Maggie, what are you doing out here?" Jaime asked, confusion written all over her face. "Don't you know we're in the middle of a blizzard? It's taken me forever to get back from town."

Jaime was in town? Then who asked me to come to her house?

"Thank goodness you saw me. My car broke down." Maggie blew out the candle, gathered her things, and locked the car. Climbing into Jaime's warm vehicle felt like heaven.

"Normally I'd drive you home, but I'm not sure we'd make it," Jaime said. "Do you mind coming to my house?"

Maggie settled back in her seat, enjoying the sensation of her limbs thawing. "Not at all. Since that was my original destination."

Jaime kept her eyes on the road, squinting into the dizzy whirl of snowflakes coming at the windshield. "Really? I'm sorry I wasn't home. I went out to do some grocery shopping when I heard a storm was coming. And I'm glad I went when I did. They were almost out of milk and bread. What can I do for you?"

"I got a text from you telling me you found more of Lillian's things and to come look," Maggie said, confused.

Now Jaime did risk a glance. "From me? I didn't send you a text."

"I'll show you when we get to your house. It must have been someone pretending to be you."

Jaime frowned. "That makes no sense at all. Why would someone do that?"

"That's what I'd like to know," Maggie said. If it was a prank, it was in pretty poor taste. She could have died. Well, maybe not, but she might have spent some uncomfortable hours stranded in the cold. Not that anyone could have known her car would overheat.

Could they?

Both women sighed in relief when Jaime pulled up the driveway and into the barn. "I'm so glad to be home," Jaime said. "At this time of year you think the worst driving is behind you, and then something like this happens." She gestured at the storm as she closed the barn door. "Let's get inside." She hurried toward the connecting door to the house.

Maggie didn't have to be told twice, although she did look around the dark barn, trying to imagine a German soldier sneaking up on Lillian while she was milking a cow. A few wisps of hay and a lingering odor of manure were the only remnants of a time when this barn had held livestock.

Jaime led Maggie through a shed with stacks of firewood, snow shovels, recycling bins and the like to the kitchen door. As they entered the main part of the house, the lights flickered. Jaime groaned. "That's what I was afraid of. We often lose power out here during storms. Tree branches come down."

She stepped into the adjacent living room, which had a woodstove connected to the fireplace. "Do you want to get a few logs?" She opened the stove door and poked at the coals, then added kindling. Flames leaped, the sticks crackling as they burned.

Maggie took the canvas carrier and made a couple of trips back and forth to the shed, filling the basket beside the stove. Then she sat on the sofa and called Emily while Jaime put on a kettle and a pot of stew, trying to take advantage of the electric stove in case the power did go out.

"Mom, where are you?" Emily's voice was anxious. "It's snowing really hard."

"Tell me about it. I'm at Jaime's. My car broke down." She decided to spare Emily the disturbing details of the prank text.

"Oh no. What happened?"

"Something's wrong with the cooling system. I'll need to call a tow truck." Maggie looked outside at the snow beating against the window. "But I doubt they'll come tonight."

"There's a warning to stay off the roads. Should we go ahead and cook the shepherd's pie?"

"Please. Eat whatever you want." Maggie peered around the corner into the kitchen, where Jaime was pulling dishes out of the cupboard. "Jaime is feeding me."

"I'm glad you're safe, anyway. Keep in touch, okay, Mom?"

"Stay warm and take care of Snickers. Love you." A pang of loneliness struck as Maggie disconnected. What wouldn't she give to be snug by the fire with her daughter? Sighing, she dialed Auld's Automotive.

Bob Auld, the shop owner, was surprised to hear of Maggie's car troubles. "I checked the fluids and filled the coolant last time you were in," he said. "What was that, a month ago? Maybe you sprang a leak. Anyway, we'll find out when I look at it."

"When do you think the tow truck will come?" Maggie asked. "Probably not tonight, right?"

Bob chuckled. "I'd say not. My wrecker is totally booked pulling cars out of ditches. And the snow is so heavy they can't keep up with the plowing. The plow truck might not get out your way until the middle of the night."

"That's what I thought. So it will be tomorrow then?"

"Let's hope so. The way it's coming down out there, we might be snowed in for days."

Oh, please, no. If such a situation arose, Maggie would find a pair of old snowshoes and hike back to town.

Jamie came into the room bearing a tray. "I thought we'd eat in here, by the stove." She set her burden on a side table. The lights flickered again so Jaime lit a few candles placed around the room. "It's not if the power's going out, it's when."

Another flicker and Jaime's prediction came true. Both women laughed ruefully.

"Good timing with the candles," Maggie said. "By the way, thanks again for taking me in. I'm sure glad I'm not still sitting in that cold car praying for rescue."

Jaime waved off her thanks. "No problem. It's nice to have company." She ferried over a bowl of beef stew and a plate holding crusty bread.

Maggie accepted the meal, placing the dishes on an end table. Picking up the spoon, she tried a mouthful. "This is really good."

The other woman settled in an adjacent chair. "I'm glad you like it. I'm not much of a cook, but I can read directions." She dug in.

Maggie dipped the bread into the stew and took a chewy bite. After swallowing, she said, "I think we're onto something with our German spy theory."

Jaime's head jerked up. "What makes you say that?"

"My daughter and her friend are interviewing William King for a school project. He lived near here during the war. He said that one of the German spies came here, to this house, while Lillian was milking a cow."

"Really? What happened?" The flickering candlelight gleamed in her eyes.

Maggie shook her head. "I don't know yet. The girls are doing William's interview in segments."

"That must be torture." Jaime broke her piece of bread in two and swirled one piece in the stew. "I'm one of those greedy types. I want to know it all right now." She laughed.

"Me too," Maggie said. "What's odd is that I haven't been able to find follow-up articles after the Germans landed. I suppose the government got involved and perhaps the outcome was classified."

"That could be," Jaime said. She stared into the fire, visible behind the stove's glass door. "Before I lived in New York, I spent some time in D.C. Let me check with my contacts there and see what I can come up with." Dimples showed when she grinned. "A lot of those old files are declassified now. With any luck, we'll learn the rest of the story."

They concentrated on eating for a few minutes, accompanied by the crackle of the wood fire and the howling of wind outside. Except for Maggie's cell phone sitting on the table and the flat screen television on the wall, the cozy scene could have happened anytime during the last century. *How many nights did Lillian spend like this, huddled beside a fire in the winter?*

Jaime broke the silence. "Maggie, I know we don't know each other well, but can I confide in you?" She cocked her head with a smile. "You're so easy to talk to."

"It's my mom experience." Maggie lightly touched her ears.

"I've learned to listen." Despite her casual words, her pulse leaped a notch. What could Jaime possibly want to tell her?

The other woman sighed. "It's Chris. I'm worried about him. He's . . . become obsessed about revisiting a family tragedy. I don't think it's wise."

"The mystery around his father?" Maggie bit her tongue. Chris had asked her to help him find Ray, but she didn't know how he'd feel about her discussing it with anyone, even his girlfriend.

Jaime looked startled. "So you know about the accident and how Ray vanished?"

Maggie shifted uncomfortably. "There aren't many secrets in a small town."

"I suppose I'm not surprised the story followed the Kings to Somerset Harbor. It was quite a scandal, even if Ronald did try to sweep it under the rug. And that's where it belongs."

"But I don't blame Chris for wanting to find Ray," Maggie said. "I would, if it were me."

"Fathers and their children." Jaime sounded sad. "Sometimes terrible events destroy what should be a wonderful relationship." She swallowed. "That accident ruined my life." She used the back of her hand to rub at her eyes. "My father was driving the other car."

11

Maggie absorbed this information, trying to assimilate it with what she knew. The article on the accident she'd read referenced the other driver, a Stewart Gates, but had been centered on the Kings. This calamity connected Chris and Jaime in a terrible way. *Is this why Jaime wants Chris to stop digging into the past? Because the Kings blamed her father for the accident that essentially destroyed Ray? What a strange turn of events that the pair met now, years later and miles away from Bangor.* A terrible idea pinged in Maggie's mind. Had Jaime deliberately moved here to find the Kings? She shoved away that notion. *Why would Jaime do such a thing?*

Jaime's voice broke into Maggie's thoughts. "It's hard to know what to say, isn't it? Thanks for listening. I don't often speak of these bad memories. To be honest, I haven't even told Chris about it yet. Is that terrible?" She didn't wait for Maggie to answer her rhetorical question. "But it wasn't just his family torn apart that night. My mother divorced my dad and changed our last name to her maiden name, Jones. She said she couldn't bear to share his last name anymore."

Maggie gave Jaime a sympathetic look. "I'm so sorry, Jaime. Sometimes awful things happen to good people. And both you and Chris have suffered." *And so have I.* She didn't often talk about her loss, but at times it helped build a bridge of connection. "I know I told you I'm a widow, but my husband died unexpectedly. He was only thirty-nine. So I can empathize."

Jaime's hand flew to her mouth. "Oh, Maggie. What an enormous loss."

"It was." Now Maggie studied the dancing flames. "But I have the memories of many years with a wonderful man. And of course, we had a daughter. She's my treasure."

"She's in college, right?" Jaime seized on this topic with seeming interest and the atmosphere in the room lightened.

A discussion of Emily took them through the rest of the stew and a dessert of apple pie and ice cream. Afterward, they loaded up the woodbox again. Then Jaime gave Maggie a flannel nightgown and made up one of the couches for her. The hostess took the other. It was decided that between the two of them, they could keep the fire fed and the house somewhat warm.

The couch was surprisingly comfortable, and Maggie drifted off to sleep to the sound of wind whistling around the eaves. She woke at around three, according to her phone, which had about twenty percent of its battery left. It was cold in the room, so she got up and stoked the fire. Peeking out through the curtains, she saw the snow had stopped. Stars freckled the inky sky.

Thank goodness. Full of gratitude, she climbed back onto her makeshift bed.

The next thing she knew, sunlight was streaming into the room and her hostess was bending over her with a cup of coffee. "Wake up, sleepyhead. We survived the storm. According to the news, we got two feet."

Running a hand through her disheveled locks, Maggie sat up and took the cup. "How nice of you. It's been ages since I've had coffee in bed that I didn't make myself."

The women shared a laugh. "Notice anything else?" Jaime pointed to a sconce on the wall. It was lit. "The power is back on. That means a hot shower."

New energy filled Maggie at this news. Living like the people of a century ago with their wood fires and kerosene lamps might sound quaint, but it was actually difficult—and cold.

Jaime lent Maggie fresh clothing, and she took a steamy shower in a warm bathroom. *Heaven.* After breakfast, the snowplow came and did the driveway, and Jaime took Maggie back to town, the wagon navigating between towering snowbanks. Maggie's car was already gone, towed to the garage.

"Here we are," Maggie said as they approached Sedgwick Manor. Fortunately, Nate Gregory, her handyman, had cleared the driveway and the walks.

Jaime whistled as they approached the house. "Wow. What a beautiful property."

"It is. I was so fortunate to inherit it from my aunt."

"I'll say. Listen, I'll come down to the shop soon. I need to find more furniture, and also some of those decorative touches that make a house a home, you know?"

Maggie paused with her hand on the door handle. "I certainly do. Would you like to come in and have coffee or tea before you go? You can meet Emily."

Jaime shook her head. "I'm sorry, but I'll have to take a rain check. I'm headed over to Chris's. We're taking Trevor on an outing."

I need to do something to thank her for her hospitality. "Why don't you and Chris come over one night for dinner? I'd love to cook you a meal."

The other woman's face lit up with pleasure. "That would be lovely. I haven't had a chance to meet many people yet, so my social life is nonexistent."

"Except for Chris."

"That's right, except for Chris." Jaime smiled. "Take care, Maggie. We'll talk soon. Oh, and I'll call my friend in D.C. tomorrow."

"I'll keep my fingers crossed that he'll be able to dig out information about the spies." Maggie shut the door and stood back to let Jaime drive off, waving and calling a goodbye.

She had barely reached the front door when it flew open. "Mom!" Emily greeted her with a big hug. "I'm so glad you're home."

Maggie hugged her back, ending the embrace with an extra-tight squeeze. "Me too. How did you girls do last night?"

"We were fine. The lights didn't go out, but we lit candles and sat by the fire anyway. It was fun being snowed in."

What is a hassle at forty is an adventure at twenty. "Glad to hear it. When are you taking off back to school?" Snickers came trotting out from the direction of the kitchen and Maggie bent to pet him. The way he pressed his head into her hand and purred, it was as if she'd been gone a week instead of just overnight.

"Right after lunch. We'll be back later this week, though, for another interview with Dr. King."

Maggie put a hand on her arm. "Guess what Jaime offered to do for us." She relayed the offer to see if government documents could be found regarding the incident.

Emily's eyes widened. "That would be awesome. Not that I don't believe William, but it's important to get corroboration."

"Now there's a big word," Maggie teased. "I guess you're learning something at that fancy college after all."

Emily laughed and put her hand on the staircase newel post. "We're studying in my room if you need us." Snickers followed her upstairs.

"Okay. I'll be puttering around down here." The house phone rang and Maggie picked up. It was Ruth.

"Good morning, Maggie. Are you free tonight? I'm having a Spam potluck dinner."

Maggie bit back a laugh. "Did you say Spam?" She hadn't heard of a dinner party built around the canned meat product before.

"I certainly did. I came across a stack of old magazines that featured quite unusual recipes. I thought we could try half a dozen or so and pick out one or two for the party. I'm asking everyone to bring a dish, except you, of course. I heard you were stranded last night at Aunt Lillian's house."

The small-town grapevine had struck again. "Yes, I was. And it was much better than spending the night on the side of the road." Maggie explained what had happened, with Ruth interjecting expressions of shock and dismay.

"I'm so glad you're all right. How fortunate Jaime came along when she did."

It certainly was, especially since Jaime was the reason I was on that road in the first place. Once again Maggie wondered who had played that awful prank on her. Only by the grace of God had she avoided injury—or worse. "I'm very grateful, believe me."

Ruth was silent a second and then she said, "Maggie can you come over a little early? I'd like to talk to you, in confidence." As scenarios flashed through Maggie's mind—Ruth was ill, she was in trouble financially, someone else they loved was either of those—Ruth went on. "I know I'm being a silly old woman, but the idea that Lillian was a traitor has been eating at me."

Maggie had been hoping to gloss over the topic of the spies until she knew more, but no such luck. "You're not silly, Ruth. It's unsettling when something turns what you think you knew about someone upside down. And yes, I'll come over early."

After promising to be at Ruth's at five, Maggie hung up and headed for the kitchen. Maybe she didn't have any Spam on hand, but she could put together a side dish to bring. She did that, then made one of Emily's favorite lunches—grilled cheese sandwiches and tomato soup.

The girls headed out after lunch, well fed and stocked with a care package of cookies, a tin of cocoa, nuts, homemade preserves, and a loaf of bread. Feeling somewhat bereft in the now-quiet manor, Maggie made a pot of tea, grabbed a book, and sat in front of the library fire with Snickers.

But she couldn't relax. After reading the same paragraph of her book three times, Maggie thrust herself out of her chair and stomped to the kitchen to make herself a cup of tea. *What am I going to tell Ruth?* As it stood, they were dependent upon the memories of a dear but failing elderly man to learn the truth about Lillian. And Barbara, with the letter to her husband and the banknote wrapper. Maggie would have to do a deeper search of newspaper archives and see if any follow-up articles were printed.

Her first search online had come up empty. She needed to visit a library or the publication itself to access microfilm or paper archives.

But that doesn't solve my problem about what to tell Ruth tonight. A comment made by her husband, a professor of archaeology, drifted into her mind: *Don't make up the missing pieces when you're putting together a puzzle. Keep looking and keep an open mind.*

. . . .

Ruth lived in a neat white ranch with blue shutters surrounded by Jersey Mac apple trees. Maggie pulled up along the curb, leaving the driveway clear for later arrivals. She picked up her bag and the dish of beets she'd made from a recipe in one of the old cookbooks and climbed out.

As Maggie stepped onto the small front porch, Ruth opened the door, wearing a floral bib apron over her clothes. She must have been watching for her. "Maggie, how nice to see you." She took the dish while Maggie shrugged out of her coat and slipped off her boots. A fluffy orange cat came running and wound itself through Maggie's legs, mewing.

Ruth laughed. "Marmalade likes you. I'm watching him for my neighbor."

"He's quite the welcoming committee."

"He sure is," Ruth said. "When you're done being greeted, hang your coat on a peg and let's go into the kitchen."

Maggie followed her along the short hall to the kitchen, passing the living room and a small dining room on the left. The dining table was already set with stacked plates, silverware, and glasses. On a sideboard stood several platters holding appetizers.

"Those just need to be warmed in the microwave," Maggie said as Ruth set the dish on the counter. "Beets and onions, from a 1940s cookbook." She sniffed. "Something smells good."

Ruth turned on the oven light to display a meat dish adorned with peaches. "One of the Spam recipes. I remember this one from childhood. It's good."

"I'm interested to try it. I don't remember ever eating Spam."

"Have a seat, Maggie." Ruth gestured toward the table, one of those tall ones with high seats. "Want coffee or tea?"

"Tea sounds good, thanks." Maggie watched as Ruth bustled around the stove, putting the kettle on to boil and pulling out mugs and an assortment of tea bags. It was peaceful in the kitchen, with classical music playing low on the radio and Marmalade purring in one of the chairs, but Maggie's chest was tight with tension. The subject of the spies was an elephant in the room.

Finally, as Ruth poured steaming water into the mugs, Maggie said, "I think Barbara Sedgwick knew about the spies. She was involved somehow."

As Ruth carefully carried the mugs over to the table, her eyes were alight with interest. "Really? How do you know?"

"I found a letter to her husband, who was a pilot serving overseas." Maggie foraged in her handbag and pulled out the envelope. After choosing a teabag and setting it to steep, she read the letter to Ruth.

Ruth's face, initially so eager, fell in disappointment. "That doesn't say Lillian was innocent. Maybe Barbara was just a bystander."

"True. But look at this." Maggie gave her the banknote wrapper, sealed inside a plastic sandwich bag. "Why did she have this? It looks like something the spies might have brought with them, wrapped around money."

"Thanks, Maggie. The notion that Barbara Sedgwick might have been in the thick of things gives me hope."

"Me too. I highly doubt that a woman married to a bomber pilot would help a German spy. So we've got to keep digging. A writer I know, Jaime Jones, is going to ask a friend in Washington, D.C., for any documents related to the case." Maggie's cell phone rang in her bag. "I'd better check this. It might be Emily."

But once again it was a number she didn't recognize, different from the prank text supposedly from Jaime. When she answered, a man's growling voice said, "What happened last night was a warning. Mind your own business."

12

At those hateful words, Maggie jumped, almost dropping her phone. As she scrambled to hold on to it, the person repeated, "What happened last night was a warning. Mind your own business." Then the line went dead.

Ruth's brows knit together. "What was all that about?"

"You heard him?" Fingers shaking, Maggie scrolled back to the call and saved the number in her contacts. "He said it twice, so I think it was a recording."

"Who would do something so vicious?"

"Hold on," Maggie said. "I've got to call my daughter." She hoped Emily wasn't being targeted too. The doorbell rang. "Go ahead and get that. When the whole group is here, I'll explain." Emily's phone rang and rang, Maggie's anxiety ratcheting up with each trill.

Finally, her daughter answered just before the call would have gone to voice mail. "Hi, Mom." Emily sounded out of breath. "Sorry, I was doing laundry and the phone was in my room."

"So you girls got back okay?" They'd sent a text but Maggie couldn't think of another pretext at the moment.

"Yes, the roads were fine. Didn't you get my text?"

"I did." Maggie forced a laugh. "I guess I missed you. It was fun having you here. Both of you."

"Gina had a blast. She kept talking about it all the way home." The last several words were drawn out humorously and Maggie laughed.

"Must have been my cooking," she said lightly. "By the way, I'm at a Spam tasting tonight."

"A *Spam* tasting? What's that?"

Maggie explained what they were doing, then said, "I won't keep you. Give me a call when you know which day you're coming back." After an exchange of good nights, Maggie hung up, swamped with relief. *So far, so good.* Whoever the prankster was, he hadn't targeted her daughter. *Yet.*

While she'd been talking, the kitchen had filled with the other members of the historical society, all bearing hot casseroles and platters. Maggie put her phone away and jumped into the fray, sliding her offering into the microwave to heat.

"Of course this wasn't standard operating procedure in the 1940s," she told Daisy with a laugh.

"Harry thought this whole thing was a hoot," Daisy said as she pulled the lid off a dish and inserted a spoon. "Then I caught him trying to sneak a taste."

Maggie eyed the confection, a square casserole adorned with triangles of meat around the edges and in a circle on top. "What is that? It smells good."

Daisy chuckled. "The recipes we picked are somewhat unusual in their presentation. That's half the fun. This one has macaroni with cream soup, diced veggies, and of course, Spam."

The array of Spam dishes on the dining room table reminded Maggie of photographs from old magazines. In addition to Ruth's loaf with peaches and Daisy's casserole, there was a bread ring with cheese dip, a macaroni ribbon loaf, and a Maine classic—baked beans topped with sliced Spam. Someone brought a big green salad, so along with Maggie's beets, there were some vegetables served. The ladies milled about, filling their plates, serving themselves hot coffee or tea or water, and chatting.

While they enjoyed era-appropriate desserts like chocolate bread custard and victory pudding, Ruth led them through a discussion of party preparations. Maggie shared finding the collection of 1940s garments in the Sedgwick Manor storeroom and her idea to have the outfits displayed at the museum when they weren't used for the fashion show. She also gave them the update about the Hoosier cabinet Jaime was donating. Finally, June said that she'd gotten a call from someone near Bangor selling 1940s kitchenware.

"Maybe you or I can take a ride up there this week, Maggie," June said.

"I'll go," Maggie said. The trip would give her a perfect excuse to visit the Bangor library to research Ray King. Then she remembered her car was in the shop. "If I have a vehicle, that is."

"What happened, Maggie?" Daisy asked. "I heard something about you being stranded?" Apparently the storm had put a crimp in the Somerset Harbor gossip network after all, because usually Daisy would be telling Maggie herself what had happened.

Maggie took them through the strange events of the night before, how she'd gotten a bogus message to go to Jaime's and then had her car overheat on the way back. Then she hesitated. How much should she share? Ruth's eyes met hers and she nodded as if to say, *Go ahead.*

Taking a deep breath, Maggie plunged in. "Remember the note in German I found? We've learned a lot more since then." She told them what the note said and about finding the banknote wrapper in Barbara's pocket, the recipe in the Hoosier, and Barbara's letter to her husband. Then she relayed the most exciting information of all—William King's interviews. "Unfortunately, William is so feeble that he can only give us very short sessions. Yesterday he left off with the arrival of the German spy in Lillian's barn!"

Even the voluble and well-informed Ina was stunned by the avalanche of information. "So you think our Somerset Harbor ancestors knew about Lillian's encounter with the spies? I can't believe my mother never said a thing to me."

"Neither did my mother-in-law, Beatrice," Deborah said. "Remember that photo album I found? She was helping the women's auxiliary with bandage rolling, scrap drives, and raising money for war bonds. Just like Ina's mother, Lillian, and Barbara Sedgwick. And I think Harry's grandmother too, Daisy. There was a Maisie Carter in the pictures."

"Yes, that's her," Daisy said. "Sweet old gal. Fortunately I got a chance to get to know her before she passed."

"So just like us, they were a tight-knit group," Fran said. "And we tell each other everything. They probably would have too."

"You haven't found anything in the newspaper archives, Maggie?" Liz asked.

Maggie shook her head. "No, I haven't found any stories after the initial one reporting that the spies landed in Maine. A news blackout, maybe?"

"And the only witness we have is a ninety-year-old man." Deborah tapped her lips with one finger. "We need to find more reliable evidence about what happened."

"I agree," June said. "Otherwise it could all be chalked up to his wild imagination."

"Since one of my relatives was involved, I want to know what happened." The look of strain was back on Ruth's face. "It's really been bothering me, the idea that Lillian might have been a traitor during one of our nation's most important conflicts."

"I can understand that, sugar," Daisy said, patting Ruth on the shoulder. "I'd feel the same way."

"Barbara's letter got me going," Maggie said. "I was already curious, but now I want to know the whole story. Oh, by the way, Jaime is going to check with a source in D.C. They might be able to locate some declassified documents on the incident."

"That's nice of Jaime to offer her help," June said. "Maybe she's planning to write a story and kill two birds with one stone."

Ruth looked even more worried, so Maggie hastened to say, "I understand your concerns, Ruth, but we're in pretty deep. I think we need to have faith and keep going to uncover the truth."

Mentioning Jaime reminded her of Chris and his request for her help. "I have something to tell you all." Maggie gazed around the table at her friends. "But it can't leave this room, okay?" They all nodded, curious and eager to hear what she had to say. "This may be why I got a threat today. Or maybe it's because we're looking into the spies."

"Come on, girl, spit it out," Daisy said. "I'm on the edge of my seat here."

"Chris King has asked me to help him track down his father, Ray. He's hoping Ray is still alive." She paused. "But his adoptive father, Ronald, wasn't supportive in the past, so Chris basically gave up. So if any of you have any ideas or would be willing to help . . ."

"We'll help you," Deborah said. "That's just heartbreaking."

"I know," Maggie said. "And he's a widower too, which makes me feel doubly terrible for him."

"Wouldn't it be great to find Ray in time for the party?" Fran asked wistfully.

"It would be," June agreed. "But rather tough. It's only days away."

The women broke into a discussion of places to look for information about Ray while Maggie took notes. Her friends were the absolute best. And if Ray King could be found, they'd do it, she had no doubt. The same was true regarding the truth about the spies.

So whoever is sending me nasty messages is out of luck. I've gone too far to stop now. If only she knew which mystery they wanted her to stop investigating.

. . . .

Maggie's brave stance took a hit the next morning when Bob, the garage owner, called. "I'm sorry to tell you this, Maggie, but your radiator had a leak." He hesitated. "And it looks like it was sabotage."

A thrill of alarm ran through Maggie. "Sabotage? What do you mean?"

"Someone punched a hole in the system so the coolant would dribble out while you were driving. Sooner or later, when it got low enough, the engine would overheat and *bam!*—you'd be stranded."

Maggie sank down on a chair, her mind whirling as she tried to grasp what the mechanic was saying. Then anger began to percolate in her belly. "I could have frozen to death. I was stranded in the middle of nowhere during a blizzard!" The implications of Bob's news were stunning. *A prank! Or something worse—an attempt on my life?* Maggie took a great, gulping breath.

"That's true, it could have been nasty," Bob said. "I think you'd better call the police. Have one of the officers stop by the garage and I'll show him or her what happened. In the meantime, I've got a loaner you can use."

"Thank you so much for your help, Bob. I'll be down in a while to pick it up." After saying goodbye, Maggie dialed Officer Robert Linton, her fingers shaking so badly she hit the wrong buttons twice. *I should put him on speed dial, I call him so often.* That tiny bit of levity helped Maggie calm enough to focus on the call.

While she waited for Robert to arrive, Maggie paced about, tidying the rooms and dusting. Housework was a good way to burn off agitation. Snickers followed, lending his assistance by perching on furniture and watching, with an occasional bat at the dusting cloth.

Finally the doorbell rang and Maggie dashed to answer. "Come on in, Robert," she said, smiling. Ina's nephew had an easy manner and a freckled, boyish face, but he was a sharp, incisive, and caring officer. Maggie had come to depend on his help whenever situations arose, as they seemed to frequently.

"I came as soon as I could. Another fender bender downtown delayed me. Happened right in front of me at the light." Robert took off his hat and ran his fingers through close-cropped hair. At Maggie's offer, he took off his thick winter jacket and hung it up, but he continued to wear his gun belt and other badges of authority.

"Want coffee? I just put some on." Maggie led the way to the back of the house, where Robert settled in the breakfast nook. She poured two mugs and set them and a plate of cookies on the table.

The officer took out his pad and pen. "Take me through it from the beginning."

Now that he was there, waiting to hear the whole story, Maggie was unable to say a word due to the tightness of her chest and the unruly thoughts jostling in her head. She couldn't figure out where to begin.

As if he could sense this, Robert looked up and met her eyes. "It's all right, Maggie. We'll get to the bottom of this."

His calm, reassuring tone pierced her distress and she felt herself relax. "How about if I give you a little background first? Otherwise the rest won't make sense." She explained about the Kings and their sad history, the shocking revelation that Nazi spies had landed near Somerset Harbor and had interacted with townspeople, and the request by Chris King to help find his father. Then she showed him the texts, told him about the voice recording, and shared Bob Auld's assessment of the damage to her car.

Robert wrote for a minute, his brow furrowed in concentration. Then he paused, still holding the pen. "That is quite a tale, Maggie.

I'd never heard about the spies before and I do want to know more. But today let's focus on the crime. Someone damaged your car and it could have resulted in grave injury—or worse—to you."

"That's about the size of it. Of course, you'll have to go to the garage and check it out for yourself, right?"

"I'll do that as soon as I leave. I'll also go talk to Jaime Jones, see what she knows about this."

"Jaime? She said she didn't send the text. It wasn't from the cell phone number she gave me."

"I'll have to look into it, but if I had to guess, the numbers that threatened you are probably both what they call burner phones, throwaways that aren't registered to anyone. But even if she didn't send the text, she might have some idea who did. So I've got to question her. Besides which, it's awfully convenient that she came along shortly after you got stranded."

Maggie hadn't thought of it that way, but he was right. She'd been so grateful to see someone that she hadn't questioned the timing. "But whoever it was wouldn't have known the weather was going to get so bad," she protested. "I certainly didn't, or I wouldn't have gone out at all."

"The snowstorm was a bonus. Being stranded when it's cold and you're far from anywhere would have been bad enough."

Again, he was right. Maggie hated to think that Jaime might be involved. She liked her, and so far she'd been nothing but helpful. *But she might have an ax to grind regarding her father.* "I don't like this, Robert."

He picked up his mug with a sigh. "I sympathize. The sooner we get to the bottom of this, the better. I'm glad you called. Things might well escalate, so if I were you, I'd keep my cards close to the chest." His smile was crooked. "I know better than to tell you to quit digging into things. So be careful."

A couple of hours later, Maggie was on her way to Bangor at the wheel of a rattling old Buick, the loaner from Bob. The thing was a boat, wide and bouncy with a tendency to float around corners.

The route took her along the coast for a while and then led north through the countryside. As she drove along back roads and sailed over rolling hills, Maggie pondered Officer Linton's advice. It might be easier to be careful if she knew what she was doing to anger someone. Today she had the excuse of a business trip, so that was the story she'd tell if anyone asked why she was visiting Maine's third-largest city.

Soon she reached the outskirts and jumped onto the highway to go downtown. The center of the city was charming, with brick storefronts and bridges over the wide Penobscot River. Her destination, Café & Collectibles, was right on Main Street, next to a chain drugstore. By some miracle, she found a spot out front, not only empty but long enough to park her ark.

Maggie hefted the big door open and got out, noting that if she did buy everything the dealer was offering, she'd have plenty of room to cart it home. As she crossed the sidewalk, she admired the window display. It featured a Hoosier cabinet like the one Jaime had donated as well as a table set with 1940s dishes, very much in the vein of what they wanted to do at the party.

"Good afternoon. How are you today?"

Maggie turned to see a man in ragged clothes leaning in a doorway leading to the rooms over the antiques store. His grin was a ray of sunshine in the middle of an otherwise quite dirty and unshaven face.

Before getting to know the men at the soup kitchen, Maggie might have quickly walked by and ignored the man, obviously down on his luck. But now compassion panged, so she said, "I'm fine. How are you?"

He raised his eyes to the blue sky, still grinning. "It ain't raining or snowing, so it's a good day."

"I hear you on that one."

Maggie fished around in her purse, but to her surprise, he shook his head. "Nope. I don't need any money. But I sure would be happy if someone would buy me a cup of coffee."

"I'll do that, since I'm going in here."

He settled back in his doorway. "I'd be most obliged. Tell April it's for Baldy." He rubbed at his wool hat, exposing a bare pate briefly. "She knows how I like it."

Maggie started walking toward the door again, then paused. "Did that drugstore used to be owned by the Kings?"

He turned and studied the building. "That's right, they did own it. That was Ronald King's flagship store, as they call it. His first one."

Baldy looked to be around the same age as Ronald, with flecks of white in his stubble and crow's-feet around his eyes. Near enough that she felt she could ask, "Do you know Ronald?"

Once again, he tugged at his knit cap, rearranging it. "Everyone knows Ronald King. Most of us enough to stay out of his way." His chuckle was raspy.

Interesting. But rather than gossip about Ronald, Maggie asked, "Did you know his brother too?"

Baldy gnawed at his lip. "Sure I did. Ray and I went to school together. Terrible what happened." He gazed off into the distance, his eyes losing focus. "Poor Ray. He had his troubles, sure. But he loved his wife, Laurie, no matter what the gossips say. Never thought they blamed the right guy for that accident. Something fishy about the whole thing."

Maggie didn't comment, hoping Baldy would say more, but he remained silent. After a moment, she said, "I'll bring your coffee in a few minutes," and headed for the door, feeling terrible about arousing obviously bad memories for the otherwise cheerful man.

Inside, a tall, slender woman in her fifties with curly auburn hair looked up from polishing a beautiful Danish console. From a quick glance around the shop, Maggie saw that everything seemed to be from the period of the 1930s through the 1960s.

She noticed Maggie studying her inventory. "Mid-century modern, they call it." She pushed a lock of hair back from her brow. "There's just something special about the style."

"You must be April. I'm Maggie, from Carriage House Antiques."

"I am. Nice to meet you. June called and said you'd be driving up. Come with me." She picked up her cloth and began walking toward the back of the shop, passing the café area to the right, which had a counter and several small tables. A server in a '50s diner uniform was dishing up soup for two women sitting at the counter, and Maggie's tummy gave an audible rumble in response to the savory odor.

"Unless you'd rather eat first," April said with a laugh.

"No, I'll be all right." Maggie remembered the man waiting outside. "I promised Baldy a cup of coffee, though."

April laughed and shook her head. "He's a character. Always hitting up my customers for a cup of coffee. Of course I don't charge them. He helps me a lot around here and it's part of his pay."

Maggie lowered her voice. "Is he homeless? I'm helping raise money for a shelter in Somerset Harbor. It's made me more aware of people in that situation."

The other woman's gaze was warm. "How kind of you. Baldy used to be homeless, but now he's living in a transitional apartment. But he still likes to hang out on the street. I think it's his way of being social."

"I'm glad to hear it." Maggie was relieved that Baldy had a place to live. He seemed like a nice man.

April opened a door at the rear of the shop. "I went to an estate sale recently and found a whole kitchen that had basically been untouched since the 1940s. I didn't need or want all of it, so I thought I'd donate some things to your auction."

Maggie wasn't sure she'd heard her correctly. "Did you say donate?"

"I sure did. William King was my doctor growing up, and he saved my life. I had scarlet fever." She opened the flaps of a cardboard box. "It'd make me happy to honor him in some small way." She threw Maggie a grin. "So you have to accept."

"Oh, I will, and we'll make sure you're credited as a sponsor," Maggie said. She'd learned that businesses appreciated recognition for their involvement in charitable events, since it doubled as advertising.

She watched, wide-eyed, as April began to unload several boxes, putting the items on a counter. First up was a series of green wooden-handled utensils, followed by Pyrex nesting bowls in primary colors, red-and-white enamel pots and pans, and a full set of Scio Hazel rose-patterned dishes.

April held up a platter. "These always remind me of my childhood."

The pattern of tiny bunches of pink, blue, and gold flowers was familiar to Maggie also. "This is an amazing amount of stuff for the auction. Frankly, I'm stunned by your generosity."

April waved a hand. "Think nothing of it. Dr. King was an important figure in my life, and I went to school with his sons and daughter-in-law." A brief look of sadness flowed over her features.

"You knew Ray and Laurie?"

She nodded. Ushering Maggie from the storage room, she said, "Let's go get some lunch. Then I'll pack the boxes for you to take."

As they settled at the counter, the server brought them glasses of water with a smile. Her name tag said *Jenna*, and she wore her short blonde hair in a ponytail.

"Jenna, I'll have a coffee and a bowl of the ham and lentil soup. What would you like, Maggie?"

"Coffee sounds great." Maggie studied the chalkboard menu behind the counter. "I'd like a turkey and avocado panini, please."

"Good choice," Jenna said, moving toward the coffeepots.

"She says that to everyone," April said.

"That's because it's true," Jenna said. "Everything here is great." Pausing in the act of filling their mugs, she looked over her shoulder with a grin. "Even if I do say so myself."

"Jenna's the cook," April said. "She suggested setting up the café in here and I've never looked back."

"It's a neat concept. We offer free coffee and sometimes cookies at my shop, but we've never considered adding a full restaurant." Maggie laughed. "Our friend Daisy Carter might not appreciate the competition, not that we'd be a match for her."

"Daisy Carter of The Busy Bean?"

"You know her?"

April added cream to her coffee. "Who doesn't? The Bean and Daisy are famous all up and down the coast. We actually buy our coffee from her. The roasts she'll let us have, not her specialties. She keeps those in-house, and I don't blame her."

The talk of coffee reminded Maggie of Baldy. "Can you please make me a cup to go? Baldy is waiting for it."

"For Baldy? Of course. He's a sweet old gent." Jenna made up the to-go cup and handed it to Maggie.

"I'll be right back," Maggie said. She hurried out of the shop. Baldy was still in his doorway, now playing a harmonica. He stopped when he spotted her. "Aren't you a dear? Thank you kindly."

"Anytime," Maggie said. "Are you hungry? Would you like lunch?"

"No thanks. I'm all set." He winked. "Jenna gave me some of that soup she whipped up today."

"Good to hear. Take care." Maggie was impressed at how the women in the shop were caring for Baldy, who was indeed a gentleman. She hoped Somerset Harbor could extend the same care and concern to the homeless and marginally housed people living there. With fresh energy to make the auction and other events a success, Maggie headed back inside.

"April, I can't get over your donations," Maggie said when she slipped back onto the stool. "They're really going to make a difference at our event."

"Tell me more. You're having a big party for Dr. King, right?"

"Yes, to celebrate his ninetieth birthday. He's also one of the last living World War II veterans in town, so we're honoring his service too."

"That sounds wonderful. And the auction is going to be held that night?"

"Yes. We found some hats made during the 1940s while we were setting up an exhibit in our museum and the whole thing grew from there. We're doing a buffet of dishes made with period recipes, a fashion show, the auction, and a dance. The proceeds are going toward our historical society and a homeless shelter."

Jenna, carrying their lunches over, heard this last. "That sounds awesome. All with a World War II theme?" She set the dishes in front of them.

Maggie admired her perfectly toasted panini, which oozed cheese. "Yes, based on Somerset Harbor during the war. William enlisted quite late, in 1943, so my daughter and a friend are making a video of his memories from the time."

"That'll be wonderful," Jenna said. "And you said there will be fashion show? I'm in."

"I hope you both can come," Maggie said. She nodded at April. "Especially since you know William. I'm sure he'd love to see you again."

"I'll plan on it. Give me the date and we'll be there." April pulled out her phone and Maggie gave her the information while Jenna went to serve a couple seating themselves at one of the tables.

"Ronald King has been great," Maggie said. "He's paying for William's party and he's also sponsoring the event."

"Maybe he's atoning for his sins." April put her hand to her mouth. "Did I just say that out loud?"

Maggie eyed her curiously. "Yes, you did."

"I'm sorry. Like I said, I knew Ray and Laurie and liked them both enormously. Their son, Chris, grew up to be a nice young man, and Chris's son seems to be a good kid. But Ronald." April shook her head. "I never could warm up to him. It's always about Ronald."

"He did take Chris in and adopt him," Maggie pointed out. "That was kind." She thought of something. "Is Ronald married? I never hear anyone mention a Mrs. Ronald King."

"No, he's never been married. No one is that dumb." Again April seemed to regret her outburst but her eyes were dancing with merriment. "Sorry. Chris, on the other hand, was married. Poor Genevieve."

And poor Chris. The man lost his mother, father, and wife. Feeling like a gossip, Maggie couldn't resist asking, "What happened? I know he's widowed, but that's it."

April swirled her spoon in her soup. "Genevieve—that was sad. She was on medication for several conditions and she had a bad reaction." April paused a moment. "You'd think her doctors would have watched for something like that while they were throwing pills at her."

"I'm so sorry to hear that. Chris and Trevor seem wonderful." *No wonder he wants to find his father. It's an attempt to redeem something out of all the tragedy in his life.*

After lunch, Maggie helped April pack the car and then drove across the river to the Bangor Public Library. There, April assured her, she would find microfilm from many of the papers in the state.

The library was a majestic structure, with tall windows trimmed with stone arches and a rotunda. Inside, marble and wood columns and spacious rooms, defined by open double doorways, gave the building a gracious air. A librarian behind the front desk directed her to the reference room. There, another librarian assisted Maggie in choosing microfilm and setting up a machine.

She started with 1943, hoping that follow-up articles about the spies had been published in some newspaper or other. But no, the story always went dark after the initial report. *By government order?* Maggie knew that during wartime, secrecy was essential. And so was preventing a panic. She could well imagine the paranoia and fear that would have arisen if the public learned of a German invasion, however covert. The government must have hoped to squash it quietly.

Maggie turned her attention to Ray King. First she searched the archives for any mention of the man and then reviewed newspaper coverage. She found the account of the accident, the initial bare-bones report. Ray, Chris, and the other driver, Stewart Gates, had been taken to the local hospital. Sadly, Laurie was dead at the scene. A later article reported that Ray had been moved to Avalon Hospital, a private facility on Mount Desert Island.

That was it for Ray. What had happened to Stewart Gates? Maggie continued scanning, halting when she read, *Local Man Charged with Vehicular Manslaughter.*

14

Her throat tight, Maggie read about Jaime's father. His lights had been malfunctioning and, in addition, his windshield wasn't clear. Both were considered negligence causing the accident, with the theory that Ray had turned because he didn't see the other car coming. Stewart had hit the Kings broadside, unable to stop due to the icy conditions.

In previous articles Maggie found, Stewart had claimed that Ray caused the accident and that he'd honked his horn when the other car turned in front of him. But soon his protests ceased and he seemed to accept his fate without a fight. He was sentenced to three years in jail.

Out of curiosity, she searched for any other coverage of the man. He'd died of cancer several years after getting out of jail. He had been unable to secure employment as a teacher again.

Maggie sat back in her chair, stunned and saddened by this story. Maybe William's preference for the distant past was due in part to the pain of the family's more recent history.

As Maggie put the microfilm away, she remembered another tragedy—the death of Chris's wife. While she was here, she might as well find out more. First she searched the indexes for *Genevieve King*. She had died five years before.

At the file cabinets, she put away the older boxes, then searched for the dates relevant to Genevieve's passing. She loaded the microfilm in the machine and found the article she sought.

The notice was brief. The young woman had died suddenly at home. That fit with April's information. Reading about his wife's untimely death made Maggie all the more determined to help Chris. If Ray King was alive, she was going to help find him.

. . . .

"I hope this will be all right for Emily's interview." Liz switched on the light to the small meeting room used by Pastor David and his board. "Fortunately we don't usually have meetings here on Tuesday nights."

"I think it's perfect." Maggie studied the room, which held a table and chairs plus a seating area with a sofa and two armchairs. An unused fireplace and tall windows trimmed with brocade curtains made the room attractive and comfortable. "The girls said it would be interesting to have different backdrops for when they edit the story together."

When Liz had found out Emily and Gina wanted to help with the soup kitchen but had another interview with William King scheduled, she'd suggested the church. They would film William and then head to the parish hall.

Liz glanced at her watch. "When will they be here?"

Maggie heard footsteps in the hall and a familiar laugh. "Right about now." She opened the door wide. "We're in here."

Emily and Gina trooped in carrying the camera equipment. Emily paused on the way by to give Maggie a kiss on the cheek, and to her delight, Gina followed suit.

Liz crossed her arms and made a mock pout. "Where's *my* sugar?" she asked in accented imitation of Daisy Carter.

Emily laughed and gave Liz a hug. "Thanks for letting us use this room."

"No problem." Liz moved toward the door. "We'll see you downstairs when you're done. We're serving meat loaf and mashed potatoes tonight, so you know what that means."

"No, what does it mean?" Gina asked.

Liz winked. "Lots of peeling." She laughed and left, leaving the door ajar. In the hallway, they could hear her greeting William and Chris. "They're in the meeting room. First room on the right."

The men entered, bringing the cold, fresh scent of the outdoors with them. After settling William in one of the armchairs, Emily gave him the signal to begin.

· · · · · · · · · · · · · · · · · ·

William King's Interview, Part 3

Lillian's shock when she saw the wounded man made her freeze. She told me later that she literally couldn't move until the cow broke the spell by bellowing in distress. Then the man said, "Milch. Gib mir milch." He gestured with a bloody hand toward the bucket and she realized what he was saying.

Reacting out of an instinctive human decency, Lillian found herself scooping up a dipper of milk and bringing it to the man's lips, holding it so it didn't spill down his clothing. Up close he smelled of sweat and blood and woodsmoke. He must have been hiding somewhere, she realized. So why was he here? Running away from the authorities?

He gulped down the milk, then leaned back against the boards, closing his eyes. "Danke." He passed right out and didn't stir, not even when Lillian shook his healthy side. Was he going to die here, in her barn?

A noise made her turn. And there I was, on Father's ancient bear-paw snowshoes, a foolish grin on my face. "Am I in time for breakfast?" My mother and younger siblings were staying with my aunt in town so Mother could get to work easily and the kids could go to school, and I had plodded over first thing to check on Lillian.

Then I saw the man, his blood-soaked sleeve, Lillian standing with a dipper in her hand. The cow bellowed again, stamping her feet.

"What's going on?" I realized I was whispering. But the sick churning in my gut told me the truth. This was one of the spies. "When did he get here? He didn't hurt you, did he?" I crossed the floor in several big strides, ready to beat the German if he'd so much as touched a hair on Lillian's head.

She put a hand on my arm. "No, William. He's hurt." She crouched down and peeled back his coat. It was stuck to his wound.

"Let me." I reached for the knife I carried. "Get me some water." Using water to loosen the cloth and my knife to cut it away, we finally got a good look at his injury. A round hole oozed blood and my stomach turned over. "He was shot."

The bullet had gone right through and by some miracle, didn't appear to have hit the bone. But the bleeding needed to be stopped.

"Help me lay him down," I said. Drawing upon knowledge I'd gleaned through books and helping doctor our animals, I cleaned and bandaged the wound, gratified to see that the bleeding slowed and finally stopped. Lillian helped me, then finished milking the cow.

She stood over me, watching as I cleaned up my supplies. "What are we going to do with him?" she whispered.

I listened to the wind howling around the barn, the sound confirming what I feared. The second wave of the storm had started. There wasn't any way to get to town or summon help.

"We'll have to keep him here until the storm is over," I said. I looked at the man, lying there with his shirt and coat cut to shreds. "Do you have anything that might fit him?"

"My father's old clothes will do." Lillian's eyes narrowed as she studied the barn walls, which had significant cracks that allowed drafts to enter. "Is there any way to get him inside? I don't think it's going to be warm enough out here." She huffed white breath to demonstrate.

"I'll have to carry him inside." I was strong, sure, but the German was large and well muscled. He wouldn't be light.

Between the two of us and the man briefly coming to consciousness, we managed to get him into the parlor. There we laid him on the sofa near the woodstove, and Lillian brought pillows and blankets. Then she found an old flannel shirt, some long underwear, and dungarees among her father's old clothes. Since I wanted to spare her the sight of the man undressed, I did the honors of dressing him. I left the dungarees off, since he was going to be in bed anyway.

Lillian was in the kitchen making breakfast, and the smell of frying Spam and brewing coffee was intoxicating to me. I was starving. Not only had I struggled to get over here *on foot to check on her, but I'd spent the last hour lugging around a spy.*

The smell must have penetrated his comatose state, because as I was tucking a quilt up around his neck, his eyes fluttered and opened. I'll never forget our first eye contact—two men who were presumed enemies but bound in that moment by our common humanity. I was the doctor, he my trusting patient.

His eyes were crystal blue, alert with intelligence. He took in my every detail, his lips quirking as though he approved. What he said next almost made me black out.

"I am a double agent." His English was slightly accented but perfectly clear.

. . . .

Maggie and the others sat dumbfounded for a minute after William stopped talking. Outside the room, they could hear the chatter of people arriving to help with the dinner. In the parking lot, car doors slammed.

"The man Lillian helped was working for *our* government?" Maggie's overwhelming emotion was relief. Lillian and the others hadn't betrayed their country after all. She and William had done the humane thing in any case by saving a man who otherwise would have bled or frozen to death.

"Mom, that was awesome." Emily's eyes shone.

"We are so going to get an A on this project," Gina said. She gave Emily a high five.

William made a gesture as he tried to rise, and Chris hurried to help him.

"Are you staying for the dinner?" Maggie asked.

Chris looked at his grandfather, who said, "I could use a hot meal about now." He shivered his shoulders. "Remembering those days, I feel cold all over again. And scared."

As the man tottered toward the doorway, giving the girls a smile and a nod, Maggie felt a stab of compunction. "I hope it's not too much for you to do this, William."

Emily winced but didn't say anything. Maggie had raised her right—an elderly man's comfort came ahead of any project or grade.

William halted and looked at them. "It feels good to get it off my chest." He tapped his chest. "I've been carrying around all these memories for decades. Now it's time to let them go." He gripped the arm his grandson offered, and the two men left the room.

"Mom, I'm so glad he's going to keep letting us interview him," Emily said. "This is a fantastic story." She unplugged her equipment and began packing it.

"I'm glad too," Maggie said. "But I felt like I had to say that. You can tell it drains him." She moved toward the doorway. "I'd better get downstairs. Potatoes are waiting to be peeled. See you in a few?"

"We'll be right behind you," Emily said.

In the main room, men were busy setting up tables. Maggie waved to James. Ronald was also there helping, along with Chris and Pastor David. The church kitchen bustled with activity, women moving back and forth in what appeared to be choreographed harmony. As Maggie entered, Liz handed her an apron. "Want to start peeling?"

"Of course. Emily and Gina will be right down to help."

"Good," Ina said, flexing her fingers. "I've already done at least five pounds." She pointed to a pile of snowy-white spuds waiting to be diced. "I'll go help set the tables."

Maggie picked up a peeler and a potato, donated by a local farmer. The flavorful Kennebec made great mashed potatoes. Emily and Gina soon joined her, and the three of them got twenty pounds of potatoes peeled, chopped, and boiled. A professional mixer whipped the cooked potatoes, and with the addition of lots of butter and fresh cream, they were ready to be served.

Daisy and June pulled multiple large pans of meat loaf and fresh rolls out of the oven, adding them to green beans and salad to complete the meal. Out in the dining room, Maggie saw that the regular crew was there, including Little Johnny, Big Johnny, and Ace. She nudged Emily, standing beside her behind the line. "That man does the best card tricks."

Emily, somehow cute despite her hairnet and plastic gloves, studied the men with interest. "I wonder what stories they have to tell."

"Me too. But poor Ace is mute."

"That's awful." Emily bowed her head and closed her eyes as Pastor David said grace. Then the line formed, moving eagerly to accept heaping plates of the delicious meal.

"Nice to see you again," Little Johnny told Maggie with a grin. His gaze landed on Emily, then went back and forth between the two. "This your daughter?"

"It is. Her name is Emily and that's her friend Gina." Maggie introduced the men.

"I have a son about that age," Little Johnny confided, his face clouding slightly. "I don't see him too often."

Maggie gave him an extra-big helping of fluffy mashed potatoes. "I'm sorry to hear that." He smiled gratefully and moved on.

Big Johnny went by, and then it was Ace's turn. "Are you going to do your tricks tonight?" Maggie asked.

Ace's eyes skittered around the room in response and his movements as he moved down the line were slow and uncoordinated. He almost tipped meat loaf and gravy on Big Johnny, who righted the plate with a chuckle. "Easy there, Ace."

"Is he all right, Mom?" Emily whispered.

"I don't know." Maggie watched as Big Johnny helped Ace to a seat at a table. "I wonder if he's ill."

More patrons came through the line, and Maggie attended to them, but she kept one eye on Ace. Something wasn't right. By the time everyone was served, she was beat. "Let's get plates and sit down, girls." Two tables at the back were reserved for volunteers.

"How are party preparations going?" James asked Maggie from his seat across the table. He'd arrived just in time to help set the tables with Pastor David.

"Great. Some wonderful vintage kitchen items and dishes were donated by a woman in Bangor."

From the next table, adjacent to Maggie's seat, Jaime Jones turned around. She had joined the Kings. "I couldn't help but overhear. Who was it?"

"April from Café & Collectibles. She gave us tons of stuff for the auction."

Jaime nodded. "I know her. She was friends with my mom." A shadow fell across her expressive eyes.

Ronald, seated beside Jaime, was listening. "We're all looking forward to the party, even Dad. Aren't you, Dad?" The older man, concentrating on his meal, didn't hear. Ronald raised his voice. "Aren't you, Dad?"

"What?" William appeared confused. "I didn't hear you."

His son's lip curled in derision, an unpleasant gesture so brief that Maggie thought she might have imagined it when Ronald covered it with a smile. Raising his voice even more, he spoke very slowly and loudly. "Are you looking forward to the party?"

At this rudeness, Jaime's expression darkened. But before she could speak, anger flashed in William's eyes. "I'm not deaf, my boy. Or stupid. Of course I'm looking forward to the party." He gestured. "All these good people have been working hard to get ready. Why they want to honor an old coot like me, well, I'm not quite sure, but I certainly do appreciate it."

Ronald tried to cover his blunder. "Why wouldn't they want to honor you? You're a decorated veteran and a retired family physician. You've helped so many people."

Maggie hid a smile. Some people were dismissive or condescending to the elderly. In William's case, such attitudes wouldn't fly. Despite his sometimes absentminded manner, he was still sharp.

She pushed back from the table, saying to her fellow diners, "Excuse me a minute, please."

When Maggie arrived at the ladies' room, she saw that others had had the same idea, so she had to wait. When she finally exited, she saw James at the men's-room door. He was trying unsuccessfully to push it open.

"Is there a problem?" Maggie asked, joining him.

He pushed again but the door stopped only a few inches in. He frowned. "Something's blocking it."

Maggie tried to peer around the door but the gap was too narrow for her head. Then she had a brainstorm. "Hold on. I've got an idea." She rooted around in her purse and found a compact. She opened it and put her arm through the opening, tilting the compact so she could see the floor.

Ace lay sprawled on the tile.

15

"It's Ace!" Maggie cried. "He's unconscious." She handed the compact to James, who peered at the homeless man lying on the bathroom floor.

James handed the compact back to Maggie. "We've got to get in there." He knelt on the floor, reaching in to push Ace's feet away from the door.

Little Johnny came down the hall, stopping short when he saw them. "What's going on?" Ladies exiting the bathroom also stopped to watch.

"Your friend passed out in the men's room," Maggie said. "We can't get in there to check on him." To the women, she said, "Ace is sick, but we've got it under control."

Little Johnny shook his head. "He must have forgotten his medication again. He does that and next thing you know, *bam!*—he's out. Some kind of heart condition." He patted his chest. "Blood pressure gets too low."

Maggie felt a trickle of relief at this news. She had feared the poor man was dead or seriously ill. "What do you do in that case?"

The other man had moved to help James, who had managed to widen the door opening. "We give him a pill, then make sure he drinks plenty of water."

Between James and Little Johnny, they got the door open far enough for both of them to sidle through. Then they moved the unconscious man to a better spot, one at each end of the Ace's body. Maggie joined them, closing the door on the curious onlookers in the hall, who hadn't taken her hint to go away.

Little Johnny crouched beside Ace and dug around in

the pockets of Ace's green Army surplus jacket. "He's always putting them in a different pocket," he said. "Aha. Here it is." He pulled a tiny unmarked metal canister from one of Ace's pockets. He unscrewed the top and removed a pill, then slid it between Ace's lips.

"Does he do this often?" James asked.

"He used to. But me and Big Johnny got on his case. It can be dangerous, passing out at random times. He might end up in the ocean or frozen to death."

"Who is he?" Maggie asked, lowering her voice to a whisper. "What's his real name?" Did Ace have a family out there somewhere wondering and worrying about him, like Liz with her uncle?

Little Johnny shrugged, tossing his long braid over his shoulder. "I don't know it. We don't share personal information, usually. Our lives before—" He made a slicing movement. "Over. All we worry about is getting through the day." He patted his friend on the shoulder. "Isn't that right, Ace?"

As if responding to Little Johnny's gesture, Ace blinked, coughed, and sat up. His eyes were white all the way around as he stared at the trio.

"Here, drink this." Little Johnny handed Ace a cup of water. "You did it again. Forgot your pills."

Ace drank obediently, handed back the empty cup, and picked up the pill container. He shook his head, then the tube, which rattled.

"Yeah, you did forget. You were passed out colder than a mackerel right here on the floor." Little Johnny handed him a fresh cup of water with a chortle. "Unless you was planning on camping out in here tonight."

The other man shook his head again as he took the water. Then he made struggling movements as though wanting to get to his feet.

"No, you sit there another minute," Little Johnny scolded. "You were just unconscious, remember?"

Someone rapped on the door and then Pastor David stuck his head in. "Everything all right in here?" His eyes filled with compassion at the sight of the stricken man, sitting up but still pale and hollow-eyed.

James explained the situation, with interjections from Little Johnny. "What we need to do is get him to bed," Little Johnny said. "Let him rest up."

"You're both booked in the shelter tonight?" Pastor David asked. At Little Johnny's affirmative, he said, "Let's get him over there then. James, can you help?"

Maggie knew cleanup was waiting, but she wanted to stay and help Ace. She'd also never been inside the shelter and she was curious to see it. "Let me tell my daughter what's going on and I'll come with you."

"The shelter is in the yellow house on the other side of the parking lot," Pastor David said.

In the dining room, people were folding the tables and chairs. Maggie found Emily and Gina in the kitchen, dish towels in hand. "Where have you been, Mom?" Emily asked. "You missed chocolate cream pie."

"I made it," Ina called. "It was lip-smacking good." She gestured at the counter where several half-eaten pies sat. "We've got leftovers."

"I'll take a piece to go," Maggie called back. To Emily and Gina, she said, "Ace is ill. But he'll be all right," she added quickly to forestall their questions. "I'm going over to the shelter with James and Pastor David to get him settled. If I'm not back by the time you're done, take the car and go on to the house. I'll get a ride with James."

"Okay, Mom. We'll say a prayer for Ace."

Maggie found her coat on the rack and slipped it on, then took the car keys to Emily. Outside in the parking lot, she got her bearings. The church parking lot fronted onto Water Way, the side street off Monroe, where the church sat. Beyond the parking lot was the yellow house, a simple but elegant foursquare structure that had once been the parsonage. Liz had told her that before they'd decided to use it, portable beds had been set up every night in another church's basement.

The porch creaked under her weight, and even in the light of the dim overhead bulb, Maggie could see both the need for repairs and the potential. A nice wide porch like this was made for rocking chairs and a porch swing, a comfortable place to sit on a summer day or evening. Perhaps she and June could find something at Carriage House Antiques to donate for just such a purpose. For now, though, dry leaves skittered on the floor and cobwebs vacant of occupants still festooned the high ceiling.

The front door was unlocked, so she went in. The front hall was papered in a faded floral print, as were the parlor and dining room to her left, but the woodwork was carved oak and the staircase a straight flight but wide and gracious. Men's voices came from upstairs, where they must already have been settling Ace down for the night. *That was fast. I guess my help isn't really needed after all.* Maggie decided to look around downstairs, not wanting to barge in on the man in his bedroom, even if it was shared with half a dozen other men.

To the right of the stairs was another room, which she guessed had once been a study or library, since it was furnished with sagging old armchairs and lined with mostly empty bookshelves. Curious, Maggie wandered in. The fireplace was especially gorgeous, adorned by a carved wood surround. On the mantel was a kerosene lantern with a pack of matches beside it. Standard-issue equipment in Maine houses, where power often failed during storms.

The book of matches was old, labeled *King's Drugstore*, from the days when stores gave out such items. Maggie turned it over, noticing that it had the Bangor address. *Interesting.* It might have been there for decades.

The men came trooping down the stairs and Maggie went to the hall to greet them. "How is he?" she asked.

"Sleeping," Pastor David said. "But I think he's all right."

"That's what he does after a spell like that—sleep," Little Johnny put in.

"I'm so glad," Maggie said.

"Look what he gave me." Pastor David held out a three of hearts card.

"That means Father, Son, and Holy Spirit according to the deck of cards song," Little Johnny said. "You being a man of God and all, I guess he thought that was appropriate."

"I appreciate it." The minister put the card back into his pocket with a smile. He asked Maggie and James, "While you're here, want to look around?"

Maggie looked at James, who nodded. "Sure. We'd love to see it."

Pastor David took them through the downstairs, explaining the remodeling they would do once they raised enough money. The dysfunctional kitchen would be modernized, and rooms in the back would become another bedroom and bathroom for clients who couldn't go upstairs. The study, living room, and dining room would also be redecorated. "We're going to be more than a shelter," he said. "We're going to connect each client with resources, so ideally they can move to their own places, and in many cases, become employed."

"In the meantime, it's a warm place for people to stay," James said.

"We are mighty grateful, and that's a fact," Little Johnny said. "I'll be helping with the project." He jabbed a thumb at his chest, which puffed with pride. "I'm not too shabby when it comes to hammering nails."

"Good to know, Little Johnny." Pastor David glanced at a wall clock. "Well, I'm going to head back to the hall."

"Us too," James said.

"I'm going to turn in," Little Johnny said. "Good night."

Outside, the trio walked across the parking lot. Pastor David said good night and headed into the hall.

"James, I told Emily to take my car and go home," Maggie said. "Can I hitch a ride?"

"Of course," James said. Then he pointed. "But isn't that your car?"

Maggie followed his finger. Emily and Gina stood near her car, which had the hood up. "What now? I just had it fixed." She hurried across the parking lot, followed by James.

"Mom, the car won't start," Emily said. "I can't figure out what's wrong."

A huge figure shambled their way. "Having trouble, ladies?" It was Big Johnny.

"We are," Maggie said. "The car won't start."

"Got a flashlight?" Big Johnny asked. Emily ran to get one from the glove box, and after he asked them a few questions and fiddled under the hood, the car roared to life.

"I'm impressed," James said.

"Me too," Maggie said. "Can I give you something?"

Big Johnny put his hands up and shook his head. "No ma'am. Glad to do it. It was simple. A disconnected wire, that's all."

"That's strange," James said, his brows knitting in concern. "How could that happen?"

"It was just in the garage," Maggie said. "Maybe something

got loosened then." An itch of unease told her that was unlikely. Bob was an excellent mechanic.

"Let me know if you need anything else," Big Johnny said. He touched his wool cap in an approximation of tipping his hat and shuffled off into the dark.

They called thank-yous after him. "Let's go, Mom," Emily said, opening the passenger door. "I'm freezing." Both girls climbed into the car.

"See you soon," Maggie said to James as she opened the driver's-side door.

"Give me a call if you have any more trouble." James tapped the roof of the car.

Maggie promised and pulled out of the parking lot. Back at the manor, she dropped the girls at the front door with the key.

"Where are you going, Mom?" Emily asked, leaning in the open passenger door.

"I'm going to park in the garage. I want to vacuum out all the salt and sand tomorrow." She didn't want to tell them the real reason—that she was concerned about vandalism. First a hole in her radiator and now a loose wire? It was too coincidental for comfort.

Emily slammed the door with laugh. As Maggie drove off, she heard her say to Gina, "She's really fussy about how her car looks. Don't eat anything messy in there." That rule had been enforced ever since a very young Emily had smeared ketchup and mustard all over new tan seats.

As Maggie halted in front of the garage, she decided she was going to park in there until whoever was behind the hostile pranks was caught. Somerset Harbor was still the kind of town where residents left keys in vehicles and doors unlocked. Maggie wasn't quite that lax, but she had apparently been careless enough to have her car tampered with twice. She didn't intend to present a third opportunity.

Feeling exactly as if she were locking the barn door after a runaway horse, Maggie secured the garage door and headed back to the house. Tomorrow she'd have Bob check over the car and make sure nothing else was wrong.

· · · · · · · · · · · · · · · · · ·

The college students headed back to school early Wednesday morning, and after dropping off her car at Auld's Automotive, Maggie walked to her shop.

"Good morning," June called as Maggie entered. "How are you today?"

Actually Maggie was a little grumpy, but she forced herself to smile. "I'm okay," she said, brushing flakes off her jacket from yet another late-season flurry. "Having car problems again though."

June paused, her hand resting on the doily she was straightening in the World War II living room display. "That's irritating. What happened?"

Maggie filled her in as she removed her coat and poured herself a cup of coffee. "So I thought the prudent thing to do is have Bob look over the car. Then I'm going to lock it up at all times and keep it in the garage."

June cocked her head. "You really think someone tampered with it at the church last night?"

"Maybe. Or sometime earlier. Maybe Bob made a mistake when he fixed it last time, but I doubt it. Fortunately the wire fell off in the church parking lot and Big Johnny was able to come to my rescue. It could have happened in the middle of nowhere." *Again.*

June frowned in concern. "So you think whoever threatened you did it?"

"I can't think of anyone else. I'll see what Bob thinks and give Robert Linton another call if need be."

The store manager bit her lip. "I was going to see if you wanted to go to Bar Harbor today for some stock. But now I'm not going to let you go alone."

"I can't anyway." Maggie gave a rueful shrug. "I don't have a car. Although I could borrow Bob's beast of a Buick again."

June crossed her arms and tapped a finger on her lips, then said, "Let me make a call and get someone to watch the store. We are going together."

"What are we picking up?" Focusing on her business would be a nice break from thinking about whoever was targeting her.

"A dealer up near Bar Harbor has a dozen or so World War II uniforms and suits. Perfect for our fashion show." June picked up the store phone and began to dial.

An idea trickled into Maggie's mind. "What's the address?"

June told her, then held up a finger, indicating that the person had answered. She spoke briefly, then thanked whoever it was and hung up. "Ruth is going to watch the store for us."

"That's really nice of her. Do you mind if we make another stop today?"

"Of course not. Where do you want to go?"

"Avalon Hospital. That's where Ray King went after the accident." Maggie had entered the hospital's address into her phone's map system and learned the facility was right outside Bar Harbor. Swinging by on the way back wouldn't take them far out of the way.

"They won't tell you anything. You know that, right?" June said.

"I know. But it makes sense to go to the last place Ray was seen. We might learn something useful."

June gave her an amused smile. "You sound like you've been reading a detective handbook."

"Maybe I'll write one," Maggie joked. She peered out the front window. "There's Ruth now."

On the way out to June's SUV, Maggie had a thought. She really should tell Chris what she planned in case he wanted to go too. Once she was inside the car and June was letting the engine warm up for a few minutes, Maggie called him. "I thought I'd stop by Avalon Hospital and see if I can learn anything about your dad," she said.

"Oh, Maggie, it's so good of you to go to that trouble." Chris sighed. "I called once and they wouldn't tell me a thing. Said something about how I wasn't authorized to have information about him."

"They'll probably do the same thing to me, but it won't take me far out of the way. Are you sure you don't want to ride up? Mount Desert Island is a beautiful place."

"I could use a diversion, frankly. But Trevor is home sick today with the flu."

"Oh, I'm sorry. I remember those days well." Taking care of an unhealthy Emily had always been heart-wrenching. All she could provide were comfort, prayers, hot soup, and cold drinks. "I hope he feels better soon."

"Thanks, Maggie," Chris said. "And keep me posted, okay?"

"I'll do that." Maggie slid her phone back into her handbag.

"Ready? Let's go." June put the SUV in gear and eased down the drive.

"Bar Harbor, here we come." Maggie settled back in the seat, grateful June had the warmers on.

This time of year there wasn't much traffic except in the middle of the towns they passed through. The vistas of bay and islands were stunning, and Maggie spotted several places she'd love to return to in better weather.

"It's a long ride but a nice one," June said. "Kurt and I spent a lot of time in Acadia National Park when the children were growing up. We'd go camping for a week, cook lobster over a campfire, and do a lot of hiking and biking."

"We did the same thing in Vermont with Emily," Maggie said. "Sans the lobster."

They shared a laugh. "We're almost there," June said. They turned onto the road leading to the island, marshes on both sides of the causeway. Another few windy miles and they were in the quaint seaside village of Bar Harbor, a tourist mecca for over a century.

The simply named Bar Harbor Antiques was on the hill leading down to the docks. June easily found a space out front. "In the summer, we'd have to park blocks away and walk," she said to Maggie.

The shop, tucked between a seafood restaurant and a gift shop, had a cozy, crowded window circled with white lights. Bells jangled as they entered, and the familiar scent of old wood, leather, and potpourri floated to Maggie's nose. The main room was crowded with furniture and household goods.

A tall, slender man wearing corduroy slacks and a warm sweater entered through an archway to the back. "June, how nice to see you again." He hurried forward and shook her hand.

"Martin, this is Maggie, the new owner of Carriage House Antiques."

Martin looked her over with interest as he shook her hand in turn. "So you're the niece I heard so much about. How do you like running the shop?"

"I love it," Maggie answered honestly. "Although Evelyn's shoes are hard to fill."

"Ah, Evelyn. She was a great lady." Martin smiled. "Can I offer you a cup of coffee or tea? That is, if you have time."

"We do," Maggie said. After the long drive she was looking forward to some refreshments. "A cup of tea sounds great."

June concurred and Martin led them through the store to

the back, where he had a combination storeroom and office. There he put on a kettle. "So tell me more about this big birthday bash you're planning."

While waiting for the kettle to boil, they filled him in. "My wife and I will have to come down," he said, handing around a basket of tea bags. "It will be fun to see my clothes in a fashion show. And Mary will love it. If you need our help backstage, let us know. We often do wardrobe duty for plays."

"What a nice offer," Maggie said. "We will need help since this is shaping up to be quite a big show. I've got a dozen or so women's outfits."

"And I've got the same for men," Martin said.

After the tea, they went downstairs to what Martin called the Clothing Cellar to see the World War II collection. Martin pulled out several suits and a selection of casual clothing, including golf and tennis outfits. Then he added an Army uniform, a pilot's bomber jacket, and a Navy uniform. The price he gave them was absurdly low and June protested.

"No, I insist. I understand it's for charity and I do a certain amount each year. I'm glad to be part of honoring a veteran. My own granddad fought in the Pacific."

"We'll add you as a sponsor, then," Maggie said.

"That's a deal," Martin said. "Now, can I interest you in a really nice breakfront I just got in? It came out of a summer cottage here on the island and was said to once belong to a Vanderbilt."

A half hour later, they were able to peel themselves away from the voluble and knowledgeable shop owner. As they loaded the SUV, June eyed the restaurant next door. "That place is supposed to have really good fish sandwiches. I don't know about you, but I'm starving."

At the thought of food, Maggie's mouth watered. "Me too."

After a quick lunch of fish fillet sandwiches and fries, they headed out of town. "Where is that hospital you were talking about?" June asked.

Maggie studied the map on her phone. "Right up here. Take a right on that side street."

Avalon Hospital was located on a dead-end road skirting the shore, in one of the summer cottages Bar Harbor was famous for. This one was long, low, and stone, with a red tile roof and extensive gardens. If not for the hospital and parking signs, Maggie thought, she could almost pretend she was stepping back into a glamorous past.

Inside the paneled reception area, a young woman sat behind a desk under a box ceiling hung with antique glass pendant lights. "May I help you?"

Maggie stepped forward. "Who can I speak to about a former patient?"

"That'd be the director of patient services." The woman shuffled papers, eyeing them suspiciously. "Who is the patient?"

"Ray King. He was released several years ago."

The receptionist gave a dramatic sigh and picked up the receiver. While she muttered into the phone, Maggie and June looked around, feigning interest in the oil paintings and potted plants decorating the room. A janitor moved a dust mop along the shiny wood floor.

The receptionist hung up the phone. "Ms. Butler will see you now." She pointed. "Third door on the left."

Maggie and June went down the hall, looking for the right door. It was almost eerily quiet in the hospital, unlike most medical facilities, which bustled with noise.

"Here we are," June said. She knocked on the door.

"Come in," called a woman's voice. Ms. Butler was thin and middle-aged, with dark hair she wore in a sleek bob. She rose to greet them, gesturing at the chairs placed in front of her desk.

"Please have a seat. How can I help you?"

Maggie and June sat down, and Ms. Butler did the same. "We're here to ask about a former patient, Ray King." Maggie bit her lip, trying to stop its trembling. She clasped her hands in her lap.

Ms. Butler cocked her head. "Are you related to the patient? Were you included in his paperwork as authorized to receive information?"

"No and no." The woman began to push back in her chair, but Maggie held up her hand. "Wait. We're not here to inquire into his medical treatment. We are trying to find him for his son and grandson's sakes. They asked us to." Maggie paused. "We're asking a post-treatment question, so to speak."

The director pushed herself back under the desk and folded her hands. "I still can't help you. If the man doesn't want to communicate with his relatives, that's his prerogative."

"There's nothing you can tell us about his plans, where he went?" June asked.

Maggie had an idea. "Did he have a friend here that we can talk to? We're his friends too, or rather friends of the family."

Ms. Butler shook her head. "I'm sorry. I have no idea if Mr. King had any friends here or not. I've only been in this job a year."

Maggie had the feeling that if she did know, she wouldn't tell them anyway. And to be fair, even private hospitals had privacy policies. With a sigh, she stood up, extending her hand. "Thanks for your time, Ms. Butler. I appreciate it."

June followed suit and they left the office. After the door shut behind them, June said, "Oh well. It was worth a shot."

As they trudged along the hallway, the janitor poked his head out of an office door. Glancing furtively up and down the hall, he whispered, "You two are looking for Ray?"

16

Maggie glanced at June. "We're looking for Ray King." She stressed the last name in case he was thinking of another Ray.

He gestured for them to step inside the office. "Hurry. We don't have much time."

Bemused, the women entered the room. "What's this about? Do you know where Ray is?" Maggie held her breath, hoping that the custodian could shed light on Ray's whereabouts.

He shook his head. "I don't know myself. But there is someone who might know." He craned his neck, peering out into the hall, then dropped his voice even lower. "A young lady visited Ray just before he left. Maybe she knows where he went. I've been working here for ten years and that was the first visitor Ray ever had that I knew of. Poor man—I thought he was alone in the world."

"A young woman?" Maggie thought of Jaime Jones. "Did she have dark hair?"

He shook his head again, dashing that idea. "Nope. She was blonde. I heard her give her name at the desk. I remember it because it's the same as my granddaughter's. Genevieve. Genevieve King."

Maggie's belly dropped with disappointment. Genevieve was Chris King's wife. And she was dead. "Thanks for this information. We appreciate it."

June thanked him too and as they hurried down the hall, eager to leave the place, she whispered, "Where can we find this Genevieve King?"

"We can't," Maggie said. "She's dead."

June's eyes widened. "What?"

They had reached the reception area, so Maggie gave June a slight warning shake of the head. Once they were outside, Maggie told June what she'd learned in the newspaper archive about Genevieve.

June connected the dots with lightning speed. "So Genevieve was the first visitor Ray had had in years. And then after she visited him, she died and he disappeared." She fished out her keys and unlocked the SUV with a double beep.

Maggie opened the passenger door. "That's about the size of it. Whether those incidents are related is anyone's guess."

"They must be," June said as she started the car. "Otherwise it's the biggest coincidence ever." She pulled out of the parking space and slowly rolled down the hospital's winding drive. "Why did you ask about a woman with dark hair?"

"Because I thought it might have been Jaime Jones. She told me that her father, Stewart Gates, was the other driver involved in Ray's accident. He went to jail for it."

"Wow." June braked at the end of the drive, absorbing this news as she waited for a couple of cars to pass. "She's dating Chris, right?"

"Yes, but she hasn't told him about the connection yet."

"Can you blame her? I could see a lot of anger going in both directions. Especially if the accident wasn't all Stewart's fault."

June's words had the ring of truth. "I think you might have hit on something, June," Maggie said. "But if Ray was also responsible, what happened to him?"

All the way home, the mystery of Ray's disappearance teased Maggie's thoughts. Different ideas and theories popped into her head, only to be argued away by her inner skeptic. They had no proof of anything after all, except what was already known.

Did Chris know his late wife visited Ray?

· · · · · · · · · · · · · · · · ·

Back in Somerset Harbor, June stopped at Sedgwick Manor to drop Maggie and the clothing off. They stowed it in a spare bedroom, where Maggie had moved the women's outfits for the fashion show, then June left to close the shop.

Maggie had three messages on her house phone. One was from Bob, the mechanic. "I can't find anything, Maggie. But I did replace the wire in case something was wrong with it." Even through the line, his puzzlement was evident. "That wasn't anywhere near where I worked on the radiator, so I honestly don't know what happened."

I do. Maggie was more certain than ever that someone had loosened the wire. The second message was from Chris, wondering if she had learned anything at the hospital. She'd call him in a few minutes, she decided, skipping ahead to the third message.

It was from Liz. "I thought you'd like to know that Ace seemed much better today. But he's taken off again. Little Johnny said he left the shelter with all his things this morning."

That was too bad. Maggie hoped the homeless man would return to the shelter and his friends. With some trepidation, Maggie picked up the receiver. She really needed to tell Chris what had happened, but she hated to discuss it over the phone.

He picked up eagerly. "Maggie. Thanks for calling. Hold on a minute." She heard footsteps and a door closed. "Did you learn anything?"

"Not exactly. They wouldn't tell me anything of course. In fact, the director of services didn't know anything. She only started a year ago."

"Oh. So it was a bust. That's too bad."

Maggie took a deep breath. "I do have one thing to tell you. A woman named Genevieve King visited Ray before he was released. Did you know that?" She didn't want to reveal that she'd learned Genevieve was his wife through her research, which might be construed as snooping.

"Genny visited Dad? No, I didn't know. I wonder why she went." He was silent for a long moment, so long that Maggie thought he'd hung up. "Maggie, I've got to do some thinking about this."

"I'm sorry if it upset you, Chris. That wasn't my intention."

"I'm not upset. Just rethinking things. Talk to you soon, Maggie. Thanks again for making the effort."

After they said goodbye, Maggie went to the kitchen to make dinner. It had been a long day, so she reheated some soup and made toast, then sat down in the library to eat, Snickers at her side and a roaring fire in the grate. She had just lifted the spoon to her mouth when her cell phone rang. Jaime Jones.

"I hope I'm not catching you at a bad time," Jaime said.

Maggie placed the spoon back in the bowl. "No, it's fine. How are you?"

"I'm doing great, thanks. Listen, I wanted to tell you that I heard from my contact in Washington. He was able to locate the files regarding the German spies." Her voice rose to a higher pitch of excitement. "One of them was a double agent, according to a letter he found. He's going to continue to look and see what else he can learn about the incident."

"That confirms what William King said in his latest interview." Maggie picked up a piece of toast and nibbled off a corner, chewing quietly. She was starving. "Emily is going to be thrilled that we can establish the credibility of William's story."

"I'm thrilled too. I think it would make an excellent feature article. I'll wait until you're done, though. I don't want to steal Emily's thunder with her project."

"I'm sure she'll appreciate that." Maggie thought of

something else. "Oh, can we count on you to help with the party? We'll be decorating and setting up the day before and could use extra hands."

"Of course. Let me know when you need me. I'm looking forward to it."

After Maggie hung up, she dug into her meal. "Let's hope that's it for the night," she told Snickers. He purred in response, stretching out and resting a paw on her leg as though to say he agreed.

. . . .

Emily and Gina arrived at about noon Thursday in a bustle of bags and excitement for the long weekend ahead. Fortunately, both of their college class schedules allowed them to take Thursday and Friday off, so they wouldn't have to make the hour drive again for a few days.

Emily gave Maggie a big hug. "I'm so glad to be here. We've got four friends coming tomorrow night to help with the fashion show. Three guys and one girl."

Maggie squeezed back, then turned to Gina and hugged her too. "Good thing I stocked the pantry and freezer." Even though they would have the buffet dinner Saturday night and could get pizza on Friday night, she knew full well how much young adults ate, especially young men.

"Dr. King is coming over this afternoon, right?" Gina asked. "I can't wait to hear what happened. I even dreamed about it one night."

"You and your dreams," Emily teased. To Maggie she said, "What can we have for lunch?"

Maggie laughed. "Turkey sandwiches and corn chowder. Once you get your things upstairs, join me in the kitchen."

After lunch, Emily and Gina set up in the library while

Maggie made a fire and prepared a tray of refreshments. To her surprise, Ronald brought William over.

"Come on in, Ronald," she said. "You haven't been here before, have you?"

"No, though I've driven past of course. It's quite the place." His eyes darted around the hallway, widening when he saw the magnificent Swarovski Austrian crystal chandelier. "Wow."

"Maybe you should get one of those for me for my birthday," William said with a chuckle. "It'd look good in my bedroom." He shuffled along, Ronald hovering nearby in case he needed assistance.

Maggie showed them to the library, where Ronald was formally introduced to Emily and Gina. "I've seen you two helping out at the soup kitchen." He darted a glance at Maggie. "Shows you were raised right." The man was saying and doing all the right things, but Maggie couldn't warm to him. Was it because she knew that he had never let Chris look for his father?

"How are Chris and Trevor? I heard poor Trevor had the flu."

Ronald stood by the fire, holding his hands out to the heat. "The boy is much better but still under the weather, so he stayed home from school again. We're hoping he'll be totally recovered for the party."

"I hope so," Gina said. "He's going to have a great time." She swooped over to William and patted his shoulder as she handed him a cup of tea. "And I bet you will too, Dr. King."

William lifted the cup to his lips, his hand shaking. "If I live to see it."

Ronald tapped his foot, shod in Italian leather, on the carpet. "Dad. Cut it out. Of course you'll live. It's the day after tomorrow."

"There were times during the war when we didn't know if we'd live through the day, let alone be able to count on tomorrow," William replied.

"That's a great quote," Emily said. "Can I write it down?"

William waved a dismissive hand. "Write down anything you want. I'm flattered you care to listen." His eyes fastened on his son. "Unlike other people."

Ronald shifted uneasily. "Oh, Dad. I've heard all your stories many times—you know that."

The older man's smile was smug. "You haven't heard the story I'm going to tell today. I've never told a living soul."

· · · · · · · · · · · · · · · · ·

William King's Interview, Part 4

Where did I leave off? Oh yes, the German had just told me he was a double agent. Naturally I didn't believe him. If I were captured behind enemy lines, I'd do the same thing, even if I didn't speak a word of German. "Prove it," I said.

"My satchel is in the barn. Look inside."

"What's going on?" Lillian appeared in the doorway. I saw her as the German must have, slender and straight, blonde hair glinting in the firelight, which played over her pretty features. "I heard two voices speaking English."

"He claims to be a double agent," I said. "We need to check his satchel. It's in the barn."

"Behind the bales of hay on the main floor," the German said.

A frown creased her smooth forehead. "Shall I go get it?"

"Please." I wasn't going to leave her alone with the German, not under any circumstances, even if he was injured.

Without argument, she turned and left, and a moment later I heard the ell door shut. "She is a pretty girl," he said. "You are sweet on her."

Apparently those clear blue eyes were pretty perceptive. I blushed and muttered something in response. Fortunately the door opened and shut again and Lillian's footsteps tapped on the floor.

"I have it," she said, holding the leather satchel by the handles. He took it from her and unzipped it. I noticed it held clothing and other items, which he shoved aside. He handed me papers.

"Hans Biener," I read. "This says you're an American citizen."

"I am. I went to Germany to offer my assistance. They didn't know I was sent by our government."

I waved the paperwork. "How do we know this isn't fake?"

"I have a contact you can talk to." Hans pointed to his wounded shoulder. "How do you think this happened? My partner found out I was working for the United States and shot me." He shook his head. "I made a mistake. Almost a fatal one."

I sat back, staring at the spy. Could I trust his words? What if he was lying? But then who would have shot him? "Do you have any other proof?"

"Like I said, I have a name you can call. I am sure he

will vouch for me." His lips twisted. "Now that the mission has failed, I am sure he is waiting to hear from me."

I looked at Lillian. She had been watching the German with narrowed eyes, reminding me of a cat studying an unfamiliar creature, not sure if it were friend or foe.

"The telephone is down," she said. "And with the snow, we can't get to town, maybe for days. Perhaps you were counting on that."

Hans closed his eyes. "I was afraid of that. I hope . . ." He was silent a long moment and I thought he had lost consciousness again or gone to sleep. Then his eyelids popped open, his eyes flashing. "You must get ready. Gunther may come looking for me." He groaned. "I am so sorry."

Lillian and I had a conference in the kitchen. "I won't leave you alone with him," I said. I still didn't trust him fully. What if he hurt her? I would never be able to forgive myself.

"But your animals. You have to go home and see to them at least."

She was right. I thanked God my family wasn't out here in the country, vulnerable to prowling spies. But it meant I had sole responsibility to milk the cows.

I finally agreed. Then I had a brainstorm. My neighbors on the other side, Doris Linton and her father-in-law, Harold, were sitting ducks if Gunther showed up. I needed to warn them, or better yet, bring them to stay with us. Harold was old—or so he seemed to me at the time—but he was strong as an ox and a good shot. Harold could help me keep an eye on Hans and be another pair of eyes to watch for Gunther.

Before I left, I bound Hans's hands and feet. The man appeared to be weak and exhausted, but I wasn't taking any chances. He was a self-admitted spy, after all, no matter who he said he worked for. Then I strapped on my snowshoes and headed out into the storm. Automobiles were useless in this weather. I'd have to hitch the draft horse to a sleigh to get back over here with Doris and Harold. Even that was going to be a tough slog.

Back home at last, I went to the barn first. My dog, Sally, was overjoyed to see me, and she licked my face while I filled her food dish. When I started milking the cows, she kept running to a side door and whining. Figuring she needed to go out, I opened it. Then I gave a yell of shock.

Footsteps cratered the snow. Someone had been prowling around.

A second look told me they were old, half-filled with new snow. I milked the cows, packed provisions that included plenty of firepower, and hitched the horse, all in a controlled frenzy. It was good practice for the Army, I told myself. Grace under pressure.

The Lintons agreed to come along without much argument since Doris was fascinated by the idea of meeting a double agent. Once we had the horse in the stable at Lillian's, she bolted inside, not even bothering to take off her winter clothing *before bursting into the parlor. I heard her shout, "I saw you the other night walking along the road!"*

Harold crowded into the room behind her. "So they were spies. I'm glad you didn't pick them up, Doris." His meaty fists clenched open and shut. "You better not give us any trouble, mister. You're in Maine now."

The spy regarded him steadily. "I am working for your government. I gave the young man my contact's name."

"So he said." Harold tapped the side of his nose. "We'll see. Until then, we're keeping an eye on you." He pulled a straight chair up beside the sofa and loomed over the other man. "Tell me about your partner. What does he look like?"

"I know that, Harry," Doris said. "I saw him."

Harold placed one of those huge hands on Hans's shoulder. "Let's see if the descriptions agree."

We listened intently while Hans described Gunther. Medium height, dark hair, a slender moustache. Doris nodded at each point he ticked off.

Harold leaned a little closer. "I'm a veteran of that little skirmish a couple of decades back. We beat you then and we'll beat you now."

"Good. I am a U.S. citizen, so I hope so," Hans said.

Sally barked outside. I had brought her along to be

our watchdog. We all stiffened, still and silent. Then she stopped, and relief swept through the room. "Must have been a critter," I said, although what creatures were stirring on a night like this? Outside, the wind rose into a frenzy, battering the old house.

"I've got stew if anyone's hungry," Lillian said.

"And I brought fresh loaves of bread," Doris added. The two women went to the kitchen. The three of us men remained quiet. I listened for unusual sounds so hard that my head rang. But we heard only the whistle of the gale.

17

William sighed and stretched, rolling his neck. "I promise I'll keep going, but I need a break."

The others, mesmerized by his tale, slowly came out of their daze. "I was on the edge of my seat," Maggie said.

"Me too." Emily reached to switch off the camera. "Your story is amazing."

"It is, Dad." Ronald appeared as stunned as everyone else. "I can't believe you never told us about it."

William leaned against the chair back, his hands resting on the arms. "I kept this story a secret for decades. But now it's time to tell it."

"Let's make fresh tea," Gina said. "And refill the cookie plate. Can I get you anything, Dr. King?"

"I'd like a glass of water," the veteran said.

"Of course." Gina grabbed the tray and left, Emily joining her.

"May I use the restroom?" Ronald asked, glancing around. Maggie gave him the directions and Ronald hurried out, making a remark about drinking too much tea.

Maggie and William were alone in the room. After a minute, she got up to put another log on the fire. As she set the poker in its place, she noticed William's eyes were closed. Concerned that they'd tired him out, she asked, "Are you feeling all right?"

He opened one eye. "I'm fine. Well, as good as you can be in your nineties. There is one thing bothering me though." He coughed, pulling out a handkerchief to cover his mouth. After a minute he said, so low it was a whisper, "I miss my son Ray." He turned his head to look Maggie full in the face.

"Chris told me you're looking for him. Can you find my son?"

The entreaty in the elderly man's eyes tugged at Maggie's heart. She wished with all her might that they could make his request come true. "I'm doing my best, William. I promise you."

"What are you promising?" Ronald stood inside the doorway.

Maggie's eyes met William's. He lowered his lids slightly, a signal clear enough that Maggie said, "I'm promising your father a very special birthday party." She attempted a joke. "I hope you like Spam."

"Love it," William said. One eyelid closed a little more, in an approximation of a wink.

. . . .

William King's Interview, Part 5

We spent a long, restless night, us men taking shifts to keep watch. Morning finally dawned, a blinding pink-and-white explosion of light.

Lillian came into the parlor. She and Doris had stayed in a small bedroom off the kitchen, close enough for protection and warmth. "I'm going out to milk the cow."

"No you're not," Harold and I said together. We looked at each other. "I'll go," he said. "I'm good at it."

I peered out the window. Maybe we could make it to town today, or at least to the nearest house that still had telephone service. The plow truck might finally get out here, now that the storm had passed.

I gestured for the others to go into the kitchen, where

Doris was fueling the cookstove. A pot of coffee was perking, the smell making my mouth water.

"Let's go to town today and take him." I jerked my thumb at the other room, where Hans lay dozing. "We need to call the authorities and get this off our backs. We can't stay holed up here forever, worrying about Gunther showing up."

"I agree," Harold said. "Let me take care of the cow, and after breakfast, we'll hitch up the horse." He stepped into his boots and shrugged into his plaid jacket.

Lillian placed pieces of bacon in a cast iron pan, releasing a delicious sizzle into the air. Doris pulled a carton of eggs out of the icebox and began cracking them into a bowl.

As for me, I retreated to the parlor to drink coffee and keep an eye on Hans. Was he friend or foe? Right now all that mattered was getting him to safety and restoring peace to our lives. Let the Feds sort it out.

"I'm out of milk," Doris said in the kitchen.

"I'll go get some from Harold," Lillian said. "Watch the bacon, all right?"

I heard the door to the ell shut. Sally stirred at my feet and gave a woof. "What is it, girl? Are you hungry?"

For some reason, a tingle went down my spine. Hans opened his eyes and looked at me. "Go."

Grabbing my rifle, I trotted through the kitchen. Doris yelped in surprise, dropping the spatula. "What are you doing, William?"

I merely shook my head in response and kept going, Sally trotting behind me, nails clicking on the floor.

We barged through the frigid ell into the barn. There a sight met my eyes that is still etched in my memory, despite the many years of war and life that came after.

Harold lay on the floor, bleeding from a wound on his head.

Across the barn, a stranger had his arm around Lillian's neck, a gun pointed to her head. Her eyes were wide with fear and pleading.

I took a step forward. Sally growled beside me.

"Do not move," the stranger said. He had a trace of a German accent. The odd thought went through my mind that they'd schooled him well. "And keep your dog back. My fight is not with you. I want Hans."

I hesitated. To give him Hans would mean a death sentence for the spy. I didn't want his blood on my hands. Besides, would this man leave us unharmed, as witnesses? That seemed doubtful.

Lillian's hand went to the breast pocket of her dress. The poor thing was putting her hand to her heart, I thought. Then I saw the wink of a diamond. Our eyes met and she gave me the tiniest of nods.

"How do I know you won't hurt us?" I asked, forcing the man to keep his attention on me. Lillian deftly pulled the pin out of her pocket, grasping it in her hand.

"My fight is not with you."

"Then let her go." I said the command again, louder, addressing the dog, "Go!"

Sally leaped through the air, a black-and-white blur, straight for Gunther's right hand. Lillian stabbed the arm holding her with all her might. He yelled and released her. She darted to one side.

Gunther screamed for me to call off the dog, who had his sleeve in her teeth and was shaking it. The little game we played so often had come in handy. Lillian grabbed the pistol, now lying on the barn floor, and trained it on Gunther, as I did the same with the rifle. Like most Maine girls, Lillian knew her way around a gun.

"Sally, stop." My dog released his sleeve but sat beside him, growling.

"Shall we tie him up, William?" Lillian said. Her eyes glittered and her hair was tangled around her shoulders. She looked like an avenging angel. She was magnificent. "I think the Feds are looking for him."

. . . .

"My aunt attacked a spy with a hatpin?" Ruth was beside herself with astonishment. The historical society was enjoying a casual Friday night supper at Maggie's after working on party preparations all day. The young adults were having pizza in the kitchen while the older folks relaxed in the library.

"William told us she kept it in her breast pocket just in case," Maggie said. "It turns out Gunther was a dangerous man, with many murders on his hands. He hit Harold with the butt of his gun and was busy stealing milk from the cow when Lillian came in. He grabbed her and was going to use her as a hostage. She ended up stabbing him with the pin as part of the plan to overpower him."

"I've read about women using hatpins in self-defense," June said. "That was good thinking on her part."

"It sure was," Ina said. "I bet my mother was sorry to miss the action while she was making bacon in the kitchen." She folded her arms, disgruntled.

"Doris is the one who took the horse to town to get help," Maggie said. "All by herself. Lillian and William were watching the spies, and Harold was hurt."

Ina brightened. "Really? Then she was a hero after all."

"She sure was," Deborah said. "I was reading my mother's journal and found an entry that talked about this episode." She opened a slender notebook. "I read this before, but it didn't make sense. Now it does." She cleared her throat. "'At the women's auxiliary meeting today at Lillian's, we heard about her unexpected visitors. Lillian found some items they left behind and each one of us got to keep a memento. She said our friendship gave her the strength to carry on during this long and difficult war.'"

"Mementos?" Ruth adjusted her glasses. "Like what?"

Maggie placed the banknote wrapper and the uniform pip on the coffee table. "Barbara had these two things."

Deborah reached into her handbag. "My mother kept this." She placed a handkerchief embroidered with the initials *HB* on the table. "It must have belonged to Hans. I never understood where it came from until now. My last name begins with *B*, but the *H* didn't make sense."

Ruth's face lit up. "Lillian had the note Hans left her, in German so no one would understand it. And the recipe."

"Yes," Maggie said, "William said they made potato pancakes for breakfast that morning before calling the authorities. Lillian enjoyed the recipe so much, she had Hans write it down for her."

"I wonder what Lillian gave my mother," Ina said. "I guess I'll have to go home and look."

"I'll ask Harry," Daisy said. "Maybe his grandmother also kept something." Daisy stretched with a yawn. "I'm tuckered out. And we've got a big day tomorrow." Daisy was leading the cooking crew, while Maggie and Ruth were in charge of the fashion show. June was handling the auction and vintage kitchen display. The others were assigned to various tasks.

The ladies helped clean up before going home, with plans to meet at the town hall midday. The party would officially begin at three o'clock.

The young people piled into the library to watch movies, and Maggie retreated to her bedroom, eager for an early night. It had been a long week. She ran a bubble bath, soaked until her skin pruned, then toweled off and crawled into bed. Snickers was already there, curled in a ball. Maggie plumped the pillows and leaned back to read.

The house phone beside her bed rang. With a groan, Maggie picked it up to see who was calling. The display said *W. King.* Instantly she was wide awake. *Is William all right?* At his age, the worst could happen any time.

"Maggie?" It was Ronald. "Sorry to bother you so late."

"That's all right. Is your father okay?"

"What? Oh, yes." He gave a little laugh. "He's fine. Very excited about tomorrow, as we all are."

"Everything is all set. Everyone worked all day to make sure that things would go off without a hitch."

"I'm sure. You're a very efficient bunch." He went silent.

He wasn't calling about his dad or the party. What is it?

"Er, Maggie. I need to confide in you about something. Please promise me it won't go any further."

Her heart began to beat harder. "Of course. I'm very discreet." Riveted, she held her breath, waiting to hear what he had to say.

"You heard about my brother, Ray, and what happened to him?"

What did Ronald know? Had he found out she was snooping around? With some trepidation, she said, "I know he was in a tragic accident and ended up in a hospital."

"That's right. It was a terrible thing, just terrible. But what people don't know is that Ray is mentally ill." He paused. "That's why I adopted Chris and discouraged him from looking for his father. He's dangerous."

18

Maggie's thoughts whirled as she tried to absorb Ronald's words. Was he telling the truth? Did Chris know this about his father? Had she been wrong to interfere? Finally, she managed to stutter, "But if he's dangerous, why did they let him out?"

"Good question. Apparently they decided he was fit to be released. Of course, it's been many years. Maybe he convinced them he was all right."

Maggie thought of something else. "Why are you telling me all this? I'm concerned for your family, certainly, but it's not really my business."

Ronald chuckled again, a low, confidential sound. "Oh, Maggie. I know you've been helping Chris look for him. I don't blame you. It would make a heartwarming story, wouldn't it? Long-lost man reunited with family. Believe me, the dream would soon turn into a nightmare if Ray does turn up. Let's pray he doesn't. Good night now."

Feeling slimy from this unpleasant encounter, Maggie was tempted to jump back into the tub and wash off. She shivered. Somehow Ronald had found out she was helping Chris. That made her feel exposed and uneasy, as if she had stuck her nose in where it wasn't wanted.

She attempted to read her book but soon gave up. After putting on a robe and slippers over her pajamas, she went out to the kitchen, where she found Emily making popcorn in the microwave. "Mom, hi. I thought you were in bed."

"I was." She sighed. "I just can't relax."

"Come watch a movie with us." Emily pulled out the bag and poured piping-hot popcorn into a big bowl. "That will take your mind off things."

"You know me too well," Maggie said with a laugh. "I have trouble letting things go sometimes."

Emily popped a fluffy kernel in her mouth. "We all do. Coming?"

Maggie joined the group of young people, none of whom seemed to mind the intrusion of a middle-aged mother. Snuggled on a sofa between Emily and Gina, Maggie relaxed, laughing along with everyone else at the absurdly funny film they had chosen.

It did the trick. By the time it was over and everyone was headed to bed, she felt delightfully relaxed and ready to sleep.

. . . .

Maggie met the other members of the historical society at the town hall at noon. Teams of people worked to complete the final preparations, including in the kitchen, where Daisy presided over the big ovens. The walk-in fridge was filled with molded-gelatin dishes, and the sizzle of baking Spam filled the air.

In two rooms annexed for changing areas, Martin and Mary, the antiques dealers from Bangor, helped make final adjustments to the fashion show outfits. Jenny from The Busy Bean was in charge of music for the show, and James had finally agreed to be the master of ceremonies after Daisy, Ina, and Ruth worked on him for a while.

"Hey, Maggie," James said as she entered the big hall, planning to check the stage. He was reading his notes by the podium. "How are you today?"

"Great, thanks. How about you? All ready for your big performance?"

He shuffled the paper with a laugh. "Sure. I have to admit I enjoy hamming it up every so often. Or should I say Spamming it up?"

It was a corny joke, but Maggie couldn't help laughing. "Good one. What's the final agenda?"

James consulted his papers while Maggie read over his shoulder. "The party starts at three. Once William is here, we're going to get him situated in that seat of honor"—he pointed to a throne—"and then we're having a color guard come in along with a parade of veterans led by Pop Welborn. Next is a performance by the high school band, then the fashion show."

"Dinner next, with cake for William," Maggie said, continuing to read over his shoulder. "Then you'll announce the winners of the silent auction. After that, the dance will start."

"That's right. We'll take a break after the auction results to clear the tables out of the hall and let the dance band set up. We got a great group that plays big band tunes out of Portland."

"Fun. Do you Lindy?" Maggie referred to the popular 1940s dance.

"No, but I heard Daisy is going to teach us."

Jaime Jones entered the hall. She spotted Maggie and James on the stage and came striding toward them, a huge smile on her face. After exchanging greetings, the writer said, "I've got a surprise visitor lined up. William is going to be thrilled."

Normally that would have been good news, but a warning bell rang in Maggie's mind. Was Jaime referring to Ray? Had she done what Chris and Maggie had failed to do and located William's long-lost son? Just a day ago, she would have been relieved and happy. After her discussion with Ronald, she was filled with trepidation about the reunion.

"Who is it?" James asked. "The governor?" Political dignitaries sometimes made appearances at community celebrations.

"No, but that would have been a good idea." Jaime searched through her phone. "Maybe I can get ahold of his office." She gave them an absentminded wave as she strolled off.

"Now I'm dying to know who she's talking about," James said. "But I guess she's not spilling the beans."

Maggie forced a smile to her lips. "It seems that way. We'll just have to wait and be surprised along with everyone else." Behind her back, she crossed her fingers and prayed Ray King wasn't Jaime's surprise guest.

At three on the dot, William arrived, escorted by his son, grandson, and great-grandson. The room was already packed and the crowd gave him a standing ovation when he appeared in the doorway. William waved as he shuffled to his seat, a throne decorated with bunting. Banners hung overhead and balloons dangled from the ceiling, which was also festooned with strings of lights.

After he was seated, drumbeats were heard and a color guard with representatives from the Legion, Eagles, and VFW entered. They were accompanied by a drum and bugle corps and parade of veterans that included Little Johnny and Big Johnny, with Pop Welborn in the lead. The sight of the Johnnies touched Maggie's heart. Everyone stood again to salute the flag, then Pastor David called out the names of other Somerset Harbor World War II veterans. As Somerset Harbor's only other living World War II veteran, Pop was seated in a place of honor near William, to roars from the crowd, who loved the retired teacher.

James got up to make opening remarks, wish William a happy birthday, and turn over the microphone to Pastor David, who invoked a blessing. The high school band squeaked and squawked out a few patriotic numbers. A local dance troupe did a series of swing dances featuring stomping feet and swinging partners around. Then Trevor got up and—with much encouragement from his father—sang his great-grandfather's favorite song, "God Bless America," in a high, sweet voice. As he sang the final verse, he approached William and handed him a small flag, then saluted him. Maggie was glad to see that hers weren't the only wet eyes in the room.

It was nearly time for the fashion show, so Maggie ducked backstage. The dressing room was a scene of barely contained pandemonium as the young women shimmied into 1940s clothing, including stockings, heels, and hats. Mary helped them zip up and fasten hooks and eyes. At a makeshift dressing table, they applied red lipstick and lots of mascara. Curling irons and hot rollers gave their hair the smooth yet curled hairstyles of the era.

"Are you serious?" one of them cried, holding up a long hatpin. "This thing looks dangerous."

"It is," Maggie said, taking it from her and inserting it into the hat to hold it on the girl's head. "It's also necessary."

"Mom, are my seams straight?" Emily turned around so Maggie could survey her calves, clad in silk stockings with the distinctive back seaming used in that period. Maggie bent and tweaked one into place.

Finally, it was time for the show to begin, announced by flashing lights and a burst of music. The first vignette featured career clothing—suits for men and women. Maggie went to the edge of the stage to watch.

To the strains of "Begin the Beguine," the couples strolled out onstage arm in arm and stopped in position. Then James gave the commentary, describing the outfits worn by each couple in turn as they walked forward, stopped, turned so the audience could see every angle of the outfits, and exited.

Accompanied by "Moonlight Serenade," the next vignette featured evening wear, dazzling full-length gowns on the ladies and tuxedos worn by the young men, who looked both proud and nervous as they escorted their beautiful partners.

Emily, with her dark hair and eyes, was stunning in creamy organza, and Maggie couldn't help but imagine Barbara Sedgwick in that dress, entertaining friends at the manor or attending a party.

She heard a deep sigh beside her and turned to see Ruth, standing with hands clasped, her eyes shining. "Seeing them reminds me of when my mother and Aunt Lillian used to get dressed up to go out. They were so beautiful I thought they were movie stars."

"We're not quite so glamorous these days, are we?" Maggie said, giving a wistful exhale of her own.

The third grouping displayed sportswear, outfits for tennis, golf, and skiing. Each couple carried the appropriate equipment thanks to someone who had located vintage rackets, clubs, and wooden skis. Emily was adorable in golfing attire consisting of baggy wool pants, a Scandinavian sweater, and a knit bonnet tied under her chin. "Swinging on a Star" provided a jaunty accompaniment.

The last vignette brought down the house. The young models wore military uniforms, including one young man dressed in William's own 10th Mountain Division pure-white winter gear. Emily and the two girls wore WAC and WAVES uniforms and the sailor suit from Sedgwick Manor.

This time, instead of posing briefly, they marched around the stage to "Over There," played by the joint military and high school bands. The crowd joined in, singing and clapping.

"Wasn't that great, ladies and gentlemen?" James said into the microphone as the models left the stage. "Next up we have a social time while our wonderful cooks set out dinner. Wish William a happy birthday and visit with your neighbors. Oh, and make your bids for the silent auction. We'll announce winners after dinner." James turned off his microphone and exited the stage.

"Coming to the kitchen?" Ruth asked Maggie.

"I will. I want to talk to Emily for a moment first."

The dressing room had the same happy sense of chaos, but now the girls were changing into pretty dresses for the dinner and dance.

"Hi, Mom," Emily called, her curls tumbling around her shoulders. "How was it?"

Maggie crossed the room to give her a hug. "It was fabulous. You all did a great job." She turned to Mary, busy straightening and hanging the vintage clothing, along with April from the Bangor antiques shop, who had come to help. "And we couldn't have done it without you two."

"It was so much fun," April said. "I adore vintage clothes." She stroked a satin dress with a sigh before hanging it up.

"We have plenty of women's clothing in our shop in Bar Harbor," Mary said.

"I'll come down," April declared. "Let's have lunch."

Maggie smiled, happy to see a new friendship develop. "I'd better get to the kitchen."

"And I've got to visit the ladies' room," April said. She followed Maggie out of the room. "What a spectacular event you've pulled together. It's wonderful to see Dr. King again. He looks great for his age."

April knows the Kings. Before she could rein in her words, Maggie asked, "Did Ray King have a mental illness?"

The other woman stopped short, her eyes widening. Then she frowned. "What are you talking about? There was nothing wrong with Ray. Not until the accident, that is."

"I'm sorry," Maggie said hastily. "I heard a rumor." *From his brother.* Had Ronald been lying, or had the family kept Ray's problems a secret?

April dismissed the whole thing with a wave of her hand. "There were all kinds of stories flying around. Especially when

Ray disappeared. People make up things to fill the gaps, you know what I mean?" They approached the women's room and April put her hand on the door. "See you in a bit."

Pushing aside her doubts and worries, Maggie tied on an apron—also vintage, as befitted the party—and dove into helping in the kitchen. Over three hundred people were attending the party, and the pile of food on the counters, in the ovens, and in the walk-in reflected that. She ferried salads to tables, piled hot rolls in baskets, and sliced too many sticks of butter to count.

"We're getting lots of bids on the antiques," June said in passing.

"You did a beautiful job with them," Liz called.

"The vignette reminds me of my mother's kitchen," Ina said. "You got it exactly right."

"We've got things handled in here, Maggie. Take that butter out to the table, and then go check out the auction," Daisy ordered.

Maggie obeyed. June had indeed gotten it exactly right. A woman was writing her name on the bid sheet while her husband watched.

The kitchen display featured the Hoosier cabinet, a vintage stove and refrigerator, table and chairs, and a counter with a sink and sideboards. A wall behind it had a window, shelving, and a clock. Pots and pans, kitchen tools and appliances, and dishes adorned the surfaces, and the atmosphere was completed by a folded newspaper beside a plate and a vase of flowers on the table.

"I feel like I can step right inside that room," the woman said to her. "I adore '40s style."

"I'm glad," Maggie said. "The auction is benefitting our homeless shelter, and most of the items were generously donated."

The woman glanced at her husband. "Hear that, honey?" She picked up the pen again and bid on another item. "Whenever we use these things, we'll remember that we helped someone by buying them."

Maggie smiled to herself. If everyone thought that way, they'd raise a lot for the shelter. Thinking of the project reminded her of Little Johnny and Big Johnny. Glancing around the room, she saw them in a corner with several other people, including someone she recognized with a glad lurch of her heart. Ace was back.

The sound of the bell Ina's mother had once used to call her children to dinner now called the partygoers to the evening meal. Maggie and the other historical society members were kept busy refilling the tables and taking care of special requests. It took a while, but everyone had a plate and something to drink and sat down, the hall echoing with chatter and laughter. The Kings sat at the head table, William in the middle, Ronald and Chris flanking him. Jaime was next to Ronald, since Trevor was beside his father, and when Maggie looked over, she noticed her frowning. Ronald made a dismissive cutting motion with his hand and Jaime turned away, staring into space with a brooding expression. *What is that all about?*

Beside her, Ruth claimed Maggie's attention and she turned back to the conversation at the historical society table. After people had their fill of the main course, they began to wander up to the dessert table. Here sat a huge assortment of cakes and pies, including many made with period recipes. Maggie noticed to her amusement that many people were avoiding the choice labeled *Eggless, Sugarless Cake*. In the spirit of the event, she took a slice.

As she walked back to her seat, she saw that Ace was approaching the head table. Only Ronald was seated there. The others were at the dessert table or mingling. Ace extended his hand to Ronald, and Maggie moved closer to see what he was holding.

Judging from its size and shape, it was a playing card. Ace turned and shambled away while Ronald stared at the card, frowning. Maggie sauntered over, trying to appear casual. "What did you get? He gave me the queen of diamonds."

His lip curling, Ronald flipped the card onto the table, faceup. It was the jack of spades. Little Johnny appeared at Maggie's elbow. He chortled when he saw the card. "Oh-ho. That's not a good one." Shaking his head, he turned to stare after Ace, who had disappeared into the crowd.

Ronald pushed back his chair with a screech of metal on wood. "It's stupid, that's what it is." He stormed off, leaving the card on the table.

"What does the jack mean?" Maggie asked.

Little Johnny leaned close and whispered behind his hand. "The devil."

19

"Why would Ace give Ronald a card with such an ugly meaning?" Maggie asked Little Johnny. Had he and Ronald had a confrontation at some point?

"I'm sure he has his reasons." Little Johnny shook his head.

"Ronald didn't get in an argument with Ace, did he? I thought Ronald was supporting the shelter with a donation."

"Is he? That's why he's been around so much. But I've never even seen them talk." Little Johnny gave a chuckle. "Not that Ace *can* talk. But he's pretty good at communicating when he wants to."

"Do you know anything about his background? Ace's, that is." Maybe the connection lay further back. A thrum of urgency began to beat in Maggie's veins. She didn't want a nasty scene to mar William's party. And in the back of her mind, she wondered . . .

"That's one of the rules of the road," the homeless man said. "We don't ask questions. It's none of our business. And the fact that someone is a drifter says enough, don't it?" He gave her a little salute. "I'm going to get me another dessert before they're all gone. See you later, Miss Maggie."

A suspicion had begun to flower in Maggie's mind, and it would not be ignored. She pushed through the crowd, looking for Chris. She noticed Trevor, playing with a group of children, so his dad should be nearby. Ah, there he was, standing off to one side, talking to Jaime.

As Maggie approached, she heard Chris say, "Your father was Stewart Gates? Why am I just finding out about that?" His tone was pitched low but Maggie heard an edge of anger in his voice.

Jaime shrugged. "There was never a good time to tell you. But when I figured out that your father was involved—"

"*My* father? His involvement was ruled an accident. End of story." Chris whirled around and charged toward Maggie. Shoulders hunched, Jaime went the other direction, toward the nearest exit.

"Hi, Chris." Maggie injected a note of cheer into her voice, hoping he wouldn't realize she'd overheard. "Isn't this a wonderful event?"

He rearranged his face into a semblance of a smile. "It certainly is." His gaze landed on his son. "Trevor is having a ball."

Maggie debated. Should she tell him her theory about Ray or wait until a better time? But she sensed things were coming to a head. She needed to tell him.

All around the hall, the throng mixed and mingled, the noise rising to fever pitch. She saw James walk out onstage. *He must be getting ready to announce the auction results.* Behind him, a group of musicians was also setting up, the big band group from Portland.

She knew she'd better hurry, before the hall became too noisy for a conversation. "Do you have a picture of your dad? More recent than the ones in the newspaper?"

He regarded her solemnly. "You think that would help find him? I'm sorry to say I don't. Ronald put all of them away. I don't even have anything beyond the old newspaper articles myself."

"That's right." Maggie bit her lip. Her gaze fell on the shelter denizens, sitting in their own circle on the other side of the room. "Do you think you would recognize him if you saw him?"

"I always thought so." His gaze followed hers to the shabbily dressed men, who wore their age and hard lives on their faces. "Oh no. You're not saying—" He looked horrified. "You think my dad is homeless?" His voice rose, attracting glances from a couple of women strolling by.

"I don't know. It's a theory." Maggie craned her neck, looking for Ace. He wasn't there. Chris's identification—or not—would have to wait.

Chris glanced at Trevor. "I'd better go check in with my son."

"I'll let you go then." Feeling as though she'd blundered terribly, Maggie poured a cup of coffee at the refreshment table and went back to her seat.

James and June began to announce the auction winners. Her group of friends cheered as each winner of the silent auction was announced. Altogether, they made a neat $8,000 from the auction. Jaime's donation, the Hoosier cabinet, was one of the most valuable items, and June made a point to thank her especially, along with the other donors.

Jaime didn't stand to be recognized, and when Maggie glanced around, she didn't see her anywhere. So she hadn't come back. Ronald hadn't returned either, or if he had, he wasn't sitting at the head table. Ace was gone too.

To her delight, she learned James had donated the stove, which was the highest-earning item. Maggie and the others hadn't known that, and they gave him a rousing cheer.

June and a blushing James left the stage, and tables were folded to make room for the dance. Lines of chairs were left along the walls.

"I'm going to the ladies' room," Maggie told Liz, who nodded. The restrooms were outside the main hall, down a side corridor and around a corner. When she got within view, she halted in dismay. A line snaked out of the room and along the corridor. Several women looked at her with amused smiles. "It'll be a while," one said.

On previous visits to the town hall, Maggie remembered that there were additional restrooms on the lower floor. Thinking those might not be as full, she hurried down the main staircase.

No one seemed to be down here. The noise and activity of the party died away as she flew down the stairs. The old building had thick walls and the hush grew deeper as she descended. At the bottom, she turned left and went through a pair of glass doors into another hallway. She scanned the closed doors for the sign she was seeking. As she spotted it, she heard a groan. Maggie froze and listened, her ears almost ringing with effort in the dead-silent corridor.

There it was again. It seemed to be coming from across the hall. Maggie tried a couple of office doors. They were locked. But the janitor's closet wasn't. She pushed open the door and switched on the light.

To Maggie's dismay, she found Jaime inside, curled in a ball, clutching her head. She was groaning.

Jaime squinted up at her. "Maggie."

Maggie barged into the room, shoving aside a mop bucket with a clang. "What happened?" She dropped to the tile floor, ignoring the pain in her knees.

"Ronald. Ronald attacked me."

Shock washed over Maggie. Why would the retired businessman do such a thing? Then Maggie remembered Stewart Gates and the car accident. "Does this have something to do with your father?"

Jaime nodded, then grimaced.

"How badly are you hurt?" Maggie asked.

"He pushed me and I banged my head, then he shoved me into this closet. I think I passed out for a while."

At that news, Maggie leaped to her feet. "I'll go get help." Head injuries were nothing to mess around with. She was grateful the local EMTs were at the party, standing by as they did during any large town gathering. A couple of officers were there too.

Jaime tried to struggle to her feet. "I'm all right."

"No, Jaime. Wait here, please." Maggie glanced around at the shelves of cleaning products. "It's not the nicest place in the world, but you'd better not get up until you've been checked."

Maggie set off at a trot, glancing ruefully at the women's room as she passed by. That would have to wait. Upstairs, she ran into Robert Linton, hovering just inside the doorway. Dancers crowded the floor beyond, cavorting to the strains of a swing tune.

"Robert, Jaime Jones is hurt. She's in the downstairs janitor's closet and needs medical attention. Bump on the head."

A look of surprise flashed over his freckled face, then he snapped to attention. "Let me get a couple of EMTs and we'll meet you down there." Discreetly, so as not to cause a public panic, Robert slipped through the crowd and tapped two men on their shoulders.

Maggie followed the three men downstairs, then quickly ducked into the restroom after she saw them approach the janitor's closet to help Jaime.

When she emerged, she found Robert standing in the hall. "Did she tell you what happened?" he asked Maggie.

"She said Ronald King pushed her and then shoved her into the closet."

Robert frowned. He pulled out his pad and made a note. Maggie thought he might ask for more information, but he merely pressed his lips together in a firm line. She was relieved, since it wouldn't be right for her to pass along details of the argument, even if she had them. Let Jaime tell the police as much as she wanted.

The clatter of footsteps in the hallway was heard and Chris appeared. "Is Jaime down here? I can't find her anywhere." His expression could only be described as haunted, no doubt a result of all the other tragedy he'd experienced.

"Yes. She is hurt, but she'll be okay, Chris," Maggie said, praying silently that she was right, and that the Somerset Harbor rumor mill didn't pick up the story. She hoped the news of

Jaime's injury wouldn't disrupt the party. "They're taking her to the hospital to be checked over."

The two EMTs backed out of the closet, bearing Jaime on a gurney. She turned to look at Chris, her eyes lighting up. He rushed to her side and took her hand. "I'm sorry," he murmured. "Forgive me?"

"No, you should forgive me," she said. "I shouldn't have sprung it on you like that."

"What happened?" Chris glanced around at the other faces. "Does anyone know?"

"Your father and I got into an argument," Jaime said. "The subject doesn't matter." A spasm of pain creased her features. "But he's on the trail of someone who might be in trouble. The man you know as Ace." She paused. "He has the crazy idea that Ace is your biological father, Ray."

Chris was visibly stunned by this news but before he could respond, one of the EMTs said, "Make way, please. We're taking her to the hospital."

Chris bent and kissed her cheek gently. "I'll see you there in a few minutes."

As soon as the medical professionals began to make their way down the hallway, followed by Officer Linton, Chris turned to Maggie. His normally pleasant face was suffused with anger and confusion. "Did you know Ace was my father?" His voice cracked on the last word.

Maggie shook her head. "No, but I did wonder if Ray was homeless. Why else wouldn't anyone know where he was? And tonight when he gave Ronald the devil card, I began to suspect he might be."

"The devil card? What are you talking about?"

"Ace communicates with people through playing cards. Remember the one he gave Trevor?"

Chris nodded. "I do. Dad was pretty upset about that. He thought the man was cracked." More confusion and misery chased over his features. He put a hand to his head. "Maggie, I'm having trouble grasping all this." His eyes widened in horror. "Do you think Dad is going to hurt Ace? I can't believe he assaulted Jaime." Bitterly he said, "He's the one who is cracked."

Officer Linton came running back down the hall toward them. "We need to find Ronald King and Ace fast." His face twisted in a grimace. "And guess what? The roads are turning into a skating rink."

"Can you gather your search party elsewhere?" Chris asked. "I'd rather this situation not be allowed to mar my grandfather's event."

Robert thought for a moment. "We can assemble at the police station," he said. "That'll be discreet enough."

"Thank you," Chris said. "I just want to check on Jaime, then I'll come back and act like all is well. It's the least I can do for Granddad."

Chris left with a short goodbye, and Maggie, James, and Robert walked over to the police station. After placing a few more calls for volunteers, Officer Linton issued an alert for Ronald's car, and teams of police and civilians departed to begin searching Somerset Harbor. The church shelter and the King home were quickly eliminated.

Maggie teamed up with James, who had his pickup truck since its knobby tires had better traction than his Mercedes. Night had fallen and the roads glistened with ice in the headlights. James crept along, careful not to use the brakes unless necessary. They had been assigned certain side streets to check for signs of Ronald or Ace. The roads were empty, everyone either at the party or sheltered inside, out of the nasty weather.

"This is like looking for a needle in a haystack," Maggie said. "Maybe we're speculating here. Perhaps Ronald isn't chasing Ace down. And it seems to me that Ace is probably really good at becoming invisible. That's what homeless people do."

James tapped his hand on the steering wheel in a rhythm. They'd traversed the streets assigned and were now down by the harbor. "I have an idea," he said. "Remember the bunker?"

How could she forget that damp, cheerless building once used to store guns? "Do you think Ace was the one staying there?"

He shrugged, waiting at the stop sign until the plow truck spewing salt and dirt went by. "It may have been him, or he might know about it. It's not that far out of town, a mile or two. He could easily walk it. I think it's worth checking."

A memory struck Maggie like a blow. She clutched James's arm. "The kerosene lantern we saw at the bunker. Remember? I saw a similar one in the shelter the other day. Along with a book of matches from King's Drugstore." Then she deflated. "Probably a coincidence."

"Maybe, maybe not." James turned onto the shore road. "Only one way to find out."

Although Maggie trusted her companion's driving, she found herself clutching the armrest on the door. Freezing rain created some of the worst driving conditions, right up there with fast-moving blizzards and mixed snow and rain, which froze into treacherous slush. As the truck's wheels crunched along, seeking traction on the ice, she found herself praying—for their safe travels, to find the homeless man whole and well, to restore Ray to the love of his family. Well, except for his brother, it seemed.

"Is that Ronald's car?" James slowed even more as they approached an Audi sedan, parked halfway in the ditch with the driver's door open. It appeared the vehicle had slid off the road and been abandoned.

"Let's find out." Maggie fished for her cell phone in her jacket pocket. "If it is, I'll call it in."

"Wait here." James halted the truck, got out, and gingerly made his way over. Ducking inside, he rifled through the glove compartment, then emerged with a thumbs-up signal and a slip of paper that looked like the vehicle's registration.

As James climbed back in the car, Maggie checked for cell service and was grateful to see she had two bars. The dispatcher put her right through to Robert. "We're out near the World War II bunker," she explained. "Ronald's car is here but he's not in it."

"Keep an eye out for him. And don't approach him, okay?" Robert said. "He could be—" The signal crackled and Robert's voice was cut off.

Maggie called the officer's name into the phone to no avail and then tried hanging up and dialing back. No connection. She shook the phone as if that would help. "At least they got the message. I'm sure they'll be right out."

Another tedious quarter mile and they reached the road leading to the bunker. This was now a sheet of ice over crusty snow but James managed to drive the truck most of the way to the end. When he turned off the engine, the sound of ice pellets hitting the windows grew louder, as did the wind tossing the trees. Maggie paused with her hand on the handle. The footing was sure to be treacherous, and she dreaded the idea of stepping outside the safe, warm cabin of the truck.

"Hang on," James said. "I have something for you." He twisted around to search behind his seat, in the cargo area. He found a small canvas bag and tossed it to her. Ice cleats.

"I'm impressed," Maggie said, undoing the drawstring and peeking inside. "These will be perfect." She pulled out an adjustable set of metal claws she could fasten on her boots.

James opened a similar bag. "I often use these or snowshoes at job sites in winter." He leaned over to put one on. "You can't depend on them being plowed or shoveled, especially if no one is living in the building."

Feet adorned, they exited the truck and began trudging to the bunker. In the short stretch of woods, the ground wasn't too slippery since the trees had caught most of the ice, their frozen branches rattling in the wind. Once they emerged into the open on the sand dunes, the icy rain smacked them right in the face, forcing them to duck their heads and squint.

"Look." James pointed to depressions in the snow. "Those are recent."

Maggie studied the footprints. They did look freshly made. And there were two sizes and patterns. She glanced up, her eyes meeting James's. "They're here." Tension coiled in her belly and her breath came short. *Are we too late?*

James squared his shoulders. "Let's go." He began picking his way along the steep slope, stamping with each step so the ice claws would hold.

The door to the old armament shelter stood partly open and as they climbed closer, Maggie saw shadows flickering on the shiny metal. She also heard shouting. James began to run, his feet struggling to find purchase on the slippery ground. Maggie gritted her teeth and recklessly picked up her pace, falling with jarring pain on one knee when her ice claw caught on a branch poking partially out of the ice. She had to use both hands to push herself upright again.

She stumbled the rest of the way to join James at the bunker's doorway. Stopped from fully opening by a pile of snow, the aperture was so narrow he had to go in sideways. "Stay behind me," he said. He stepped inside. Sticking close to him, Maggie sidled through.

The scene that met her eyes was horrific, accentuated by the long black shadows dancing on the concrete walls.

Ronald King stood over a cowering Ace, holding a long needle at the man's neck.

20

"Ronald, put that down." James's voice thundered, echoing in the hollow room.

Ronald flinched with a twitch of his shoulders but he didn't lift the needle. Ace turned a pleading gaze on his rescuers.

"I'm serious, Ronald. The police are on their way. Do you really want us to be witnesses to murder?"

Still not moving the syringe, Ronald turned his head. An ugly sneer sat on his features. "I'm not murdering him. I'm putting him out of his misery."

"Like you did to Genevieve?" The sound of her voice startled Maggie. She hadn't planned on saying anything, especially not about what she merely suspected: That Ronald had silenced Genevieve after learning she visited Ray. James threw her a wide-eyed look of surprise. She held up her hand. *I've got this.*

Only a shudder down the retired pharmacist's spine revealed that her words had struck a nerve. "I don't know what you are talking about. This man is terminally ill. With cancer. He wanted me to help him die."

Ace chanced a slight movement, a subtle shake of his head.

James edged closer to the two men, stepping silently across the floor.

"It's the old story of Cain and Abel," Maggie found herself saying. "The jealous brother. Is that it, Ronald?"

That arrow hit its mark. Ronald lurched away, the needle still held like a dagger in his hand. "No. I was never envious of Ray. But I couldn't let anybody find out I was driving that night. I would have lost my license to practice. I'd worked so hard, I was so close, just passed the exams—my life would have been ruined."

Behind him, Ace tipped an invisible bottle to his mouth, the universal gesture for drinking. Now it all made sense. "You were inebriated that night. So you ran away and left Ray to take the blame." Then she had another thought. "And you had another victim. Stewart Gates. Was it really his fault? Or did you just hound him into submission?"

Ronald made a scoffing sound. "Stewart. What a loser. He didn't even fight back."

"How many lives have you ruined with your greed?" Maggie mused. She pretended to count them off on her fingers, keeping the man's attention on her. "Let's see. Your brother and his wife. Your adopted son and his wife. And let's not forget Trevor. Then there's Stewart and his daughter, Jaime . . ." Meanwhile Ace and James traded looks.

"You don't know what you're talking about." Ronald's face was red with anger, his voice strangled. "Ray was hurt in the accident, he needed care. I had to pay for it somehow—"

"An accident you caused."

"I was fine to drive, I told them. I only had a few."

"So you bullied your way to driving that night?" Maggie shook her head, unsurprised. In the corner of her vision, she noticed James tensing. She made sure to maintain eye contact with Ronald so he wouldn't notice.

Ronald roared and charged forward, the hand with the syringe raised. As one, the other two men tackled Ronald, knocking him to the ground, James in front, Ace in the rear. Ronald grunted and yelled, flailing with his fists, but he was no match for the younger, stronger James, who pinned him with ease. As for Ace, he collapsed, sitting with his head in his hands.

Maggie hurried to his side. "Are you all right, Ace? Or should I call you Ray?"

He gave a tiny nod, then—to her dismay—passed out flat on the floor.

"James. What should we do?" Maggie felt the pulse in his neck. Weak but steady. Little Johnny had said Ray had low blood pressure. Had he forgotten his pills again?

"I can't do much at the moment," he said, his voice strained as he fought to keep Ronald contained. "Look for something to tie this guy up, okay?"

Maggie rummaged around the homeless man's knapsack, locating a couple of straps used to tie on a sleeping bag and tent. She brought them over to James and helped him secure Ronald's wrists and ankles.

"You won't get away with this," the man blustered. "I'm well connected. I'll charge you with assault and battery."

"And Jaime Jones will charge you," Maggie said quietly.

That shut him up. James went over to Ray and hunkered down beside him. He lifted his wrist to take his pulse. "So this is the mysterious Ray King. Under our noses the whole time."

Maggie turned to regard Ronald, then looked back at his brother. Take away the long, greasy hair, the unkempt beard, add a few pounds—yes, she could see the resemblance to the picture in the newspaper. William, Chris, and Trevor would be so happy to see him. Maybe it would mitigate the pain Ronald's betrayal would cause when they found out.

Men shouted outside. "The cavalry are here," she said.

James nodded. "Figured they'd get here when it's all over but the shouting."

Ronald had heard them too because he began to yell, "Help! Help me! Somebody help me!"

"What'd I tell you?" James grinned at Maggie.

• • • • • • • • • • • • • • • • • •

The painted lady looks lovely tonight, Maggie thought as she walked toward the Queen Anne that housed the historical society. Lights gleamed in every window, and through the glass, she glimpsed a crowd of elegantly dressed guests chatting and laughing.

Tonight was the reception for the World War II exhibit and, by coincidence, the first day of spring. Surprisingly, the weather had cooperated, the snow and ice of a week ago melting away like ice cream in the sun. The air wasn't quite warm, but the world was thawing, releasing odors of earth and dormant green things.

Inside the door, Maggie took off her gloves and slipped out of her best wool coat.

"May I take that for you?"

She turned to see James, handsome in a suit, his hand outstretched. "Yes, thank you." She handed him the coat, then straightened the skirt of her red dress. "You look nice tonight."

"And so do you." He deftly placed her coat on a hanger. "I like your hat."

Her hand went automatically to the capulet topping her curls. "Really? I'm still getting used to it. Ruth insisted we all wear them."

"And they are spectacular." James's nod was solemn as he gazed at the approaching Daisy, who wore a confection of violets edged with a fetching veil.

"Sugar, I'm so glad to see you." Daisy leaned in and gave Maggie a hug. "Jaime Jones has a surprise for us, she said. Do you know what it is?"

Maggie raised her eyebrows. "Not a clue."

James shook his head. "Don't ask me. I have no idea what you're talking about."

The night of the birthday party, Jaime had told Maggie she had a surprise. Maggie had assumed the reporter had located Ray King. But that hadn't been it, apparently.

"I've got to get back to Harry, but I'll see you." With a wave, Daisy sashayed away, the skirts of her purple dress swaying.

"Shall we take a tour?" James asked Maggie. "I've been around once, but it's worth a second look."

"Of course." Maggie had helped set up the exhibit but there was nothing like seeing it through the eyes of visitors. As they entered the main room, she saw William King standing with Chris, Trevor, and another man, all dressed in suits. When this last person turned, she saw it was Ray King. The change in his appearance was so startling, she gasped. His hair was neatly trimmed and his clean-shaven jaw revealed a somewhat gaunt but attractive face.

"He's a handsome fellow, isn't he?" James said in a low voice. "Cleans up good, as they say."

Ray's eyes met Maggie's and he nodded. She detoured over to greet them, both joy and trepidation in her heart. It was thrilling and wonderful that Ray had been reunited with his family, but also tragically sad how the separation had come about in the first place.

Ronald had been arrested for his attacks on Jaime and Ray, and there was little doubt he'd be convicted for both. He'd also admitted tampering with Maggie's car, hoping to scare her into dropping the search for Ray. But under the advice of his attorney, he'd refused to say anything further and even recanted his confession from the night in the bunker. He continued to deny being in the car with Ray and Laurie and that he had anything to do with the death of Chris's wife, continuing to assert that her deadly medication combination was an unfortunate accident. At the time Genevieve had gone to visit Ray in the hospital, Ronald insisted that he had been negotiating the sale of the drugstore chain. Coincidence or not? Jaime's father had told her he thought there was another passenger in the car, presumably Ronald, but because Stewart was dead, her testimony counted for nothing.

Ray of course held the key, as he had since the beginning. His injuries had made it simple for his brother to tuck him away, ensuring that he had enough prescription drug treatments to keep him confused and passive.

Maggie recalled the heartrending conversation she'd had with Chris a day or two after Ray was identified. "Maybe he can't talk, Maggie, but he can write. He told me that Genny showed him a picture of Trevor. When he saw him, he became determined to get out of the hospital and try to come back into our lives. He stopped taking his medicine, except for the heart drugs, and checked himself out. But being 'on the outside' was harder than he realized. And he was afraid of Ronald, afraid he'd kill him, as he'd threatened to do so often."

Maggie's heart squeezed with compassion. "So he came to Somerset Harbor to see if he could at least keep an eye on you and Trevor?"

"Exactly." Chris's eyes had shone with tears. "I still can't believe I have my father again. But I have to be honest, it's hard wrapping my head around what Uncle Ronald did."

He was Uncle Ronald now. And last Maggie had heard, Ray refused to testify against his brother. He felt the family had been through enough.

All this went through Maggie's mind as she walked up to the Kings. She greeted William first. "Have you recovered from your party yet? I've never seen such a bash."

William chuckled. "I'm happy to say I haven't. That was the party of a lifetime."

"I danced all night," Trevor said, gazing up at Maggie with bright eyes. "It was fun."

"He did," Chris said. "Put the rest of us old fogies to shame."

"That one's a regular Fred Astaire," William said. He snapped his fingers and shuffled. "I used to cut quite a rug myself."

Trevor's laughter pealed out. "Cut a rug? What's that?"

William, still snapping, turned in a circle. "Dancing, my boy, hoofing it up."

Everyone laughed. Chris turned to Maggie and James. "I'd like to introduce you to my father, Ray King." Pretending they hadn't met in a desperate situation on a stormy night, he introduced them. Playing along, they all shook hands.

"I heard you're showing my interview tonight," William said, preening. "Your old great-grandfather is a movie star, did you know that, Trevor?"

The boy's eyes grew wide. "Really? That's awesome."

Maggie looked around. "Where is the screening?" Emily and Gina had come over earlier to set up equipment for watching the edited interview.

"In the dining room," James said. As if on cue, the lights flickered and everyone began to move in that direction.

The dining room table had been moved out and rows of folding chairs set up. Maggie and James chose to stand at the back, allowing older people the luxury of a seat.

Emily and Gina were at the front of the room, clutching notes and regarding the crowd with anxious expressions. Maggie gave them a little wave and a thumbs-up. The girls smiled back. Emily stepped forward. "Ladies and gentlemen, thank you for coming tonight for the premiere screening of *Operation Hatpin*."

A chuckle ran around the room at the title. Emily waited for it to die down, then introduced Gina, who gave an overview of the project. Gina then introduced William, "the star of tonight's film." The video started, beautifully edited interviews interspersed with photographs of the people involved and Somerset Harbor, and screenshots of news articles and declassified documents regarding the affair.

The audience was rapt, held in thrall by William's incredible tale, with gasps and exclamations at the appropriate places. When the credits rolled, the audience broke into hearty applause. Emily and Gina took a bow, then made William come up for one of his own. The older man smiled widely at the accolades. After a few minutes, he held up a hand. The crowd quieted.

"Thank you, everyone, for your interest," William said. "But I'm merely the bearer of the story. It's sad to realize that I'm the only person left who was there in the farmhouse that night—"

"That is not true, William," came a voice from the doorway. Everyone turned to stare, necks craning in curiosity. Whispers fluttered along the rows.

Maggie, who was standing nearby, had a good view of the visitor. The man was of medium height and very old, with wispy white hair and brilliant blue eyes. Jaime stood behind him in the hallway, arms crossed and a satisfied smile on her face. So this was her surprise.

William squinted, puzzled. "I'm sorry, but who are you?"

Emily nudged Gina, who held up a phone to capture this encounter.

The man took another step. "Don't you recognize an old friend? I am Hans Beiler. The spy who did *not* get a hatpin in the arm." The onlookers laughed.

"Hans? Is it really you?" William's eyes filled with joy. "I never knew what happened to you. They took you away and I never heard from you again."

"They had to give me another identity and hide me. My cover was blown." Hans shook his head. "I helped translate German in the code office. After the war, I became Howard Bean, a dairy farmer in Kansas. I had all the milk I could drink and never had to steal any again." Again the throng laughed.

As president of the society, Ruth stepped in. "On behalf of

the historical society, I would like to welcome you to Somerset Harbor, Hans. I trust you didn't sneak in this time?" Her comment provoked more merriment.

Hans bowed graciously. "That is right, ma'am. I came by air, not sea. Thank you for your kind welcome. I am very happy to be back."

"I'd like to suggest we adjourn for coffee and cake and let William and Hans catch up. But first, let's give our young film-makers another round of applause for taking the time to capture this important piece of our town's history."

"What a wonderful surprise," Maggie said to Jaime after the group dispersed. "This is really thrilling." Ruth had joined William and Hans, no doubt sharing memories of her brave aunt. Emily and Gina were also surrounded by an admiring crowd.

Jaime's smile was wide as she threaded her arm through Chris's. "Once we found the declassified documents, it wasn't that hard to find him. And I was ecstatic to learn he was still alive."

"Thanks for doing that for him," Chris said. By the look in his eyes as he gazed at the reporter, Maggie guessed young Trevor would have a new stepmother soon.

James offered her his arm. "Cake and coffee?"

"I'd love some," Maggie said, slipping her arm through his.

As they made their way toward the refreshment table, greeting friends as they went, Maggie's heart soared with happiness. The hard Maine winter was behind them at last. March had gone out like a lamb, the lion finally vanquished.